P9-BYA-247

benilde little

good hair

a novel

•

scribner paperback fiction
PUBLISHED BY SIMON & SCHUSTER

SCRIBNER PAPERBACK FICTION
Simon & Schuster Inc.
Rockefeller Center
1230 Avenue of the Americas
New York, NY 10020

First Scribner Paperback Fiction edition 1997
SCRIBNER PAPERBACK FICTION and design are trademarks of
Simon & Schuster Inc.
Designed by Karolina Harris
Manufactured in the United States of America

7 9 10 8

The Library of Congress has cataloged
the Simon & Schuster edition as follows:
Little, Benilde.
Good Hair : a novel / Benilde Little.
p. cm.
I. Title.
PS3562.L78276G66 1996
813'.54—dc20 96-26013
CIP

ISBN 0-684-80176-0
0-684-83557-6 (Pbk)

For Clifford, for being true,
and for Baldwin

A C K N O W L E D G M E N T S

There isn't enough room to thank all the friends and family who have helped me along the way, by listening, encouraging, or taking me out to eat on their expense accounts. You know who you are.

There are some musts: Thanks to my parents, Clara and Matthew Little, for giving me courage and pride and to Mom for babysitting beloved Baldwin. Thanks to the stalwarts: Wendy Rountree, Linda Villarosa, Valerie Wilson Wesley, Sharon Joni Brown, Eleanore Wells. Thanks to Abigail Thomas for her magic and the workshop crew. Thanks to Monique Greenwood, Lynne Scott, Kim Hubbard, Shannon Ayres, Jill Nelson, Irene Neves, for the sisterhood. Thanks to June Chisholm, Ph.D., who cheered this on when it was an embryo, and to Harold Jackson, M.D., who helped me to picture a surgeon's life. Thanks to Lori Merritt for Afrotiques. Thanks to my computer men, "big" Cliff Virgin and Jimmy Spence. Thanks to Joan Virgin for understanding. Thanks to Stephanie Stokes Oliver at *Heart and Soul* for giving me work, and to Susan Taylor and my *Essence* family for giving me wings. Thanks to my friend Ronald D. Brown, Esq., for his writer's ear and heart. Thank you to Cassie Jones for guiding the manuscript through the canal and to Christine Saunders and the rest of the Simon & Schuster Publicity Department for getting the word out. Thank you to my editor, Dominick Anfuso, for seeing what I was trying to say and getting me to say it. Thank you to my husband, Cliff, for giving me and my art a home, for resolute support, and for wanting to read my work every day. An enormous thank you to my agent and friend, Faith Hampton Childs, who has run this marathon alongside me with grace, intelligence, and grit. And for hosting book parties: Monique and Glenn Greenwood-Pogue; Michael and Christa Doren; Danny Meachum; Jocelyn Winston; Alvin Kendall; Mercedes Riley Terry and the Houston Links; W. Michelle Terry; Sharon Joni Brown; Lori Woolridge and Lynne Toye; Rita Sillas and Terry Lee; Stephanie Culpepper and the Deltas; Jackie Boyden and the Morris County Links; Beverly and Raymond Ransom; Clara and Matthew Little; Joan and Clifford Virgin; Siobhan Teare and Carolyn Ryan Reed; Marge Baskerville; Vernon and Vera Alleyne.

"If you bring forth what is within you,
what you bring forth will save you.
If you do not bring forth what is within you,
what you bring forth will destroy you."

JESUS, The Gospel of Thomas

LIFE IS FULL OF people who are dead. Empty people who don't know what's wrong with them or, in the most severe cases, that there is even something wrong.

When I'd met Miles, right after Mount Holyoke, I was one of those people. I had been living in Manhattan for five years, hanging out with a bunch of women who, in addition to sharing an alma mater, shared a 1950-ish goal of "marrying well." It was actually a phrase that we used to describe what we all wanted: a Black Ward Cleaver, who made a million dollars a year and dressed in Armani.

•

What these prized stallions would want in return from their wives-to-be seemed doable at the time: constant stroking, a happy disposition, and great hair—which meant long but requiring little artificial maintenance.

I had met Miles Browning at a party. He smelled my hollowness and zoned in on me like a coyote on a campfire. The party was a typical Manhattan one, where the price of admission is a blue-chip résumé. The lights were low and the dhurrie was rolled up and stashed in a corner. Sade crooned under a din of Buppies getting down, but not too hard, while playing Negro Geography—who-do-you-know and where-did-you-go-to-school.

"So, are you as bored as you look?" Miles said after we'd been introduced by the host.

I watched him pour himself a plastic cup of Freixenet, his merino wool turtleneck and gray flannel slacks sculpting every part of his perfectly muscular frame, and smiled. "No, actually, I'm rarely bored at these things."

I amused myself by listening in on other people's conversations. It continually amazed me that everybody knew everybody else and if they didn't directly, then they always knew someone in common. One needs only two pieces of information in order to place someone—where they grew up and where they went to school. Sometimes only the school is needed.

I was dressed in a below-the-calf Lycra knit black dress, black tights, and thick high-heeled black pumps. Large baroque pearls punctured my earlobes, and a thin gold bangle dangled around my hand. My shoulder-length hair was relaxed, hard.

"I like what you're wearing," Miles drawled.

"Thanks." I was too overwhelmed by him to say more.

"So you here wit somebody?"

"No. I came by myself."

•

Miles raised an eyebrow, an obvious gesture to indicate he thought me daring. He was intrigued, but misled. I was not daring, I merely felt comfortable going to the party alone because I was a casual friend of the host, a Steve Urkel look-alike who had had a crush on me. I was attracted to Miles in the most base fashion, and even though he was handsome in a Joe Morton way, his looks weren't the appeal. There was something else about his deportment that said he was a little bit dangerous, not in a gun-in-the-silk-sock kind of way, but like a ghetto Gordon Gekko, an unscrupulous manner. The fact that he was also an investment banker held equal appeal. He was going to be my Ward.

Miles grew up poor in Memphis and used his Tennessee accent the way a cat used cunning. The thicker he turned it on, the more he wanted something though in his work there was barely a trace of Tennessee. "I got enough strikes against me," he'd joke whenever I teased him about the Main Line lockjaw he adopted at the office. He piloted a red Porsche Carrera convertible, wearing cognac-colored driving gloves around Manhattan as if he were the baron born, and I fell for him and all the trimmings.

After two dates he invited me to go with him to Paris for a week. "I know you the one, baby," he told me on our second date over a bottle of Lafite-Rothschild 1962 at the Four Seasons. "We just need to get outta New York and spend some real time together." I was convinced that I was in love with Miles, and I made a deal with myself at that moment to do whatever I had to do, which turned out to be pretending to be someone else, to close the deal. I'd anointed him the perfect man: Ward doing the levels—eatin' ribs with the brothers who work for transit and drinking Veuve Clicquot with CEOs.

In our first year together, I literally put my best face forward, rising before he did, which meant predawn, to wash my face and brush on custom-matched Prescriptives face powder. I would search *The Wall Street Journal* for mergers and acquisitions I could discuss with him, and I routinely sent him tokens—sterling cuff links from Tiffany, Armani sunglasses—when he closed a big deal or had to work through a weekend. Even though these trinkets cost almost my weekly salary and I was barely covering my rent, car insurance, and student loans, I was on a mission to get him. My best friend from high school, Cheryl, thought I was on my way to a mental hospital. That was pathetic enough, but to Cheryl the clincher was that I got up before Miles to put on mascara. "Anybody you had to do all that for—before even having coffee—wasn't worth having," was her opinion.

She was right, but she was also part of the living and part of my past, the one I didn't value. The one that I had once wanted to hide.

My name is Alice Andrews. I was named after my father's mother, Alice Eliza Andrews. A fancy name for a sharecropper's wife, isn't it. She was. He wasn't. My father's parents grew up in the South, South Carolina. I didn't know them, they were dead when I was born, and even if they hadn't been, I have a feeling I probably wouldn't have known them very well. My mother's side was the dominant force in my life.

I was born to a woman who was born of a woman of prodigious will. My grandmother Viola packed up two daughters in South Carolina, leaving behind a job in some White family's kitchen and a dead husband. She would go to Elizabeth, New Jersey, without a job, an education, or a place of her own to stay.

In the 1930s Black people were leaving the South like ducks at a skeet shoot, clutching hearsay about factory jobs and northern streets that were literally paved with gold. They moved north, in Jim Crow train cars or hitching a ride in someone's old car, in the dead of night for fear of landowning Whites persuading them, at rifle point, to stay. Grandma Viola was big boned, stood about five feet eight, and had broad shoulders. Her caffè latte complexion and what the old folks used to call "good hair" gave fodder to her air of superiority. Her hair alone was something most Black folks were proud of in those days because it was proof that your heritage was mixed with Indian and/or White and you were therefore better than those coil-knotted Black people who were unblended, unadulterated. However, Grandma Viola's family, especially her daddy, was ashamed of the whiteness in the blood because it was evidence of the White man's violation of Black women and of the Black man's impotence to protect them.

Her hair and her stature gave her the appearance of confidence that made many rural Blacks and Whites uncomfortable. People used to say, "Viola don't take no tea for the fever," which means she didn't take any stuff from people. At the slightest provocation, she would tell someone to go to hell or to kiss her ass. People would say that she was full of herself. Actually, though, she was full of shame. Shame about the way she looked and the way her own people valued those looks, which were the result of a violation of spirit as well as body. Her daughters, my mother and Aunt Thelma, inherited her spirit and probably her shame. Some have said that they passed it on to me. I know I got the good and the bad.

The North turned out to be a harsh life, and Grandma Viola became bitter. Not only were the streets not coated with gold, some of them weren't paved at all. The only factory jobs given to Blacks were the worst of tasks, like sweeping furnaces and floors, and even those weren't easy to get. Grandma Viola took in laundry and made sure her kids hustled for odd jobs. By the time my mother got to high school, she had a full-time job doing daywork for a barely middle-class White family in Union. Her humiliation at having to wear her pink maid's uniform underneath her school clothes and her own mother's indifference to her shame was something she'd spend a lifetime trying to overcome. Grandma Viola was concerned about survival, and my mother's paycheck was part of the palliative. My mother had been a bright, athletic student, earning mostly A's in high school and a spot on the girls' track team.

"Roberta, that runnin' ain't gon' put a thing on this table," Grandma Viola would say.

Track was forgotten, but my mother kept her grades up, lugging her books with her to the White folks' house in Union, studying Hawthorne while her young charges practiced their scales, reciting Blake and Tennyson as she peeled potatoes for dinner.

She was convinced that her good grades were to be rewarded with a better life and a chance at going to college when she overheard a conversation between Grandma Viola and her sister, Aunt Estelle, during one of Estelle's visits north. Estelle had stayed in South Carolina, gone to Atlanta University, and become a teacher. She and her husband could not have children, and Aunt Estelle told Grandma Viola that she would pay for my mother to go to college if she maintained her grades. Before my mother could burst into the kitchen to thank Aunt Estelle, she heard her mother's voice.

"Roberta's gotta work, Estelle, ain't no use in you fillin' her head wit a bunch of yo' highfalutin talk. What she look like goin' to college, anyway? She ain't nothin', and all the college in the world ain't gon' change that." Standing outside the family apartment, in the hallway, my mother felt the walls closing in on her. She convulsed into tears so heavy that they soaked the front of her pink maid's uniform. For her, she would later tell me, in that moment she was forced to let go of her dreams for herself. It was as if all her ambition were frozen, put into a capsule, to be defrosted for me.

•

"I vowed that my daughter would want for nothing, the least of which would be a college education."

Once my mother learned to swallow her fate and realized that what awaited her was what most girls her age had to look forward to—a career as a domestic—her grades dropped, and by the eleventh grade she'd gotten pregnant and had to drop out of school. A shotgun wedding was held in the living room of my grandmother's apartment, and seven months later she had a stillborn child. Ten years later, my brother, Lucas, was born. Just about two years later, I came.

My mother was a scrupulous housekeeper. Everything in our house was immaculate: the folds in the lampshades, the cracks behind the radiators, me. My mother always made sure that I looked my best, that our house was the cleanest in the neighborhood. She turned a spare room in our three-story, two-family house into an ironing room, where she pressed our sheets, her bras, my father's boxer shorts. Looking back, I believe it was her therapy. She'd present a perfect picture to hide the mess that was inside. My third-grade teacher, Mrs. Silver, once asked me who did my shirts. She assumed we had a maid. I didn't understand what she assumed, so I asked my mother who did our shirts. My mother rolled her eyes and didn't answer. Mrs. Silver told the other teachers that we had a maid, and they all watched what I wore to school, checking the label of my beige cashmere to see if it actually came from Lord & Taylor, and commented that we were an unusual Negro family to know about quality of this kind. My reversible corduroy jumpers were fussed over by the teachers—primarily striving first-generation college-educated Jews from the same South Ward neighborhood. They were kind to me, pinched my cheeks, and commented about how pretty I was. Yet I was totally confused by their accolades, because I hated my clothes. I wanted to dress like the kids from the projects who wore the trendiest clothes, like wet-look jackets and gauchos from Lerner's.

We were the only family on the block that didn't have plastic covering the furniture. We had slipcovers. We had rugs, when everyone else had nothing, or else the latest wall-to-wall. We had heavy drapes that made our house feel like a cocoon in the fall and winter; others had shades or multicolored polyester curtains. My bedroom, however, was my mother's decorating tour de force. It was a replica of Gidget's, TV's reigning American princess in the 1960s. I had the white colonial bedroom furniture set—desk, dresser, chest of drawers, bookcase, and canopy bed with the floral bedspread and canopy cover. I was about eight when the Bamberger's delivery truck pulled up in front of our house, and I remember thinking that adults were very strange to get this excited about something as uninteresting as furniture. My mother was glowing. But, I guess, for a woman who never had her own bed, much less her own room, this was a very big day for her. She spent weeks hand sketching and painting little daisies on the walls and choosing just the right fussy sheer white curtains. She got on her hands and knees, applied chunks of wax, and then machine-buffed the hardwood floors till they gleamed.

"You are everything I ever wanted to be," my mother would say to me almost daily. So the piano and dance lessons that she had shuttled her former charges to and from were now provided for me. The expensive, conservative clothes worn by the wealthier White kids whom her sister, Aunt Thelma, took care of were the clothes she bought for me. The French schoolgirl's hat and matching coat, the beige cashmere with the velvet collar, the reversible green plaid jumpers, the whole Hahne's, Lord & Taylor, stock were hanging in my closet.

I wasn't born when my family moved into our gray frame house at the mouth of the Weequahic section in 1950. Then Newark's South Ward was where you moved up to, especially if you were Black—it was the Upper East Side, and the Weequahic section was its Park Avenue. Parts of Weequahic were just starting to open up to Black people, and my family was the first one in the neighborhood. Realtors wouldn't sell houses to Blacks beyond Lyons Avenue, which was the entrance to the Weequahic Park area, where English Tudors and large Dutch colonials were set back from the maple-lined streets called Vassar and Goldsmith. Each decade a fresh immigrant success moved in and the old families moved out. First there were the WASPs, who began moving out in the 1930s and 1940s as the Irish moved in; the Irish began moving out in the 1950s as the Jews moved in. The Italians had established a separate haven, in the North Ward, where they still live. When my parents bought their house, east of Lyons, it was on a pretty block of mostly two-family homes, with brick-front porticoes and wrought-iron railings. Large maples lined the block and the houses were painted yellow, pink, and green, and ours was gray, with a white picket fence around the small front yard, where my mother planted red and yellow tulips. My father built matching fencing around our backyard, which was big enough for a patio, a large walnut tree where our basketball hoop hung, and two fairly long plots of grass and two sets of hedges. My brother, Lucas, and I played with the Germans, Cubans, and Jews in the neighborhood. My dad, a navy veteran who fought in the Pacific during World War II, worked at the post office on some kind of assorting assembly line, and my mom was home all day. We were sort of like the family in *Father Knows Best,* except a tan version, and it was my mother who usually had the answers. We were living the American dream, I thought.

When Sidney's family moved in, the second Black family, he was five, I was four, and he became my best friend. Sidney's father

•

walked with a limp because of an old college football injury. He was a high school football coach and a jock of all trades. Sidney had no interest in sports. He and I played house. I wanted him to be the daddy, but he refused and claimed one of the baby dolls from the pile resting on my pillow at the head of my bed as his baby. "I'm a mommy, too," he announced to me, and put my brother Lucas's plastic typewriter cover over his head as a wig. We drank Tang from my toy china cups with our pinkies extended.

More families like ours moved in: the Hallmons, the McKnights, the Browns. The Schnitzers and later the Kauffmans moved out. Our neighborhood had an Our Gang quality. All these families had kids. The McKnights had nine and were newly arrived from Georgia. The Hallmons lived in our second-floor apartment, and my mother and Mrs. Hallmon would talk for hours on the back stairway. The fathers bonded under open car hoods. In the warm months, the neighborhood girls, me, and Sidney, who was always with me, moved from porch to porch, playing jacks and Barbies and jumping French and double Dutch. The boys, Duke, Cool Breeze, and Icky Harold, teased Sidney, called him a fag or a sissy fag for always hanging around with girls. He'd give them the finger while jumping flawless French. I loved Sidney. We'd sit on my porch until we'd see his mother, whom he called by her first name in front of her, coming up the block, rushing in, to cook dinner before his father got home. It was Sidney's cue to go home.

In summer yellow pylons were put at each corner and our parents would have block parties. Sidney would win the one-legged races and eat too many hot dogs. In winter the grown-ups had cocktail parties at each other's homes and would bring their kids already dressed in pajamas. I loved wearing my light blue footies. The parents would let us stay up and watch the action, which was loud talking over riffs of Nancy Wilson and Otis Redding or dancing to Johnny Taylor and Wilson Pickett. They drank Johnnie Walker Red. The kids would fall asleep and stay till the next morning. It was the kind of neighborhood where people didn't lock their doors. The husbands had factory or government jobs, and most of the wives worked as secretaries, teacher's aides, or nurse's aides, or in one of the many city factories like RCA or Singer, or as sales clerks at places like Bamberger's. We didn't need phones because people would just drop by. I thought we'd live in this safe, warm place forever or at least until we grew up and went away to college, which in my house wasn't ever an option, but a mandatory exercise, like getting christened.

By the time I got to the sixth grade the 1967 riots happened. The riots devastated the Central Ward, and that changed my world forever. Suddenly my preppy clothes, the furniture in our house, my piano lessons, became a topic, something that separated me from the new, less fortunate kids who were moving into my neighborhood from the Central Ward. Nothing about me or my clothes had been an issue with kids on my block, I guess because everybody was pretty much the same. At first the change was imperceptible. White people had moved out overnight, selling their beautiful Tudors and colonials for peanuts, but most of them were in the Weequahic Park section anyway. They'd left my block years earlier. What began happening was that some of our family friends, some of the ones who didn't own their houses, began moving away to places like East Orange, Orange, and Irvington. The new families who moved into the surrounding blocks were different because there was just a mother and two, three, or four kids. If there was a father, he was usually a father of one of the kids, the youngest one, not the whole family. The new families had several different last names taped to their mailboxes. They ate things I'd never heard of, like mayonnaise sandwiches, with no bologna or salami. It was just mayonnaise spread on two slices of Sunshine white bread, but Sidney and I didn't let those things stop us from making friends with our new neighbors. We introduced them to some established traditions, like playing jacks on the porch, jumping French and double Dutch. At school, however, I was surrounded by new and hostile faces. Sidney—who was a year ahead of me—was busy trying to pretend to be butch and to like softball in order to keep from getting beat up by the new tough boys. The new girls decided that I "thought I was cute" and didn't like me. I never could figure out how they could tell what I thought since I always thought my thoughts, everyone's thoughts, were private. Actually, what I was really thinking was that I wanted to be like them. To be able to chew gum and make it crack. To be double-jointed, so that instead of my legs looking straight up and down, they curved backward. At first it was just one or two girls who had moved from the Central Ward, who would pick on me and threaten to "beat me up after school." Then the gang of girls wanting to fight grew, and by seventh grade, I was dealing with a new threat every day, learning to live with a permanent fear of being attacked. I tried making friends with the new girls at school, inviting them to my house at lunchtime and after school for snacks. Pam, a heavy new girl with a good disposition and leadership skill, was the only one who came. We played with my Barbies and watched the Monkees on my thirteen-inch Motorola in my room, then she went back and told the other girls what my room looked like. The new girls started calling me "White girl" and saying that I thought I was better than they. In 1968 calling a Black person White was equivalent to callin' their mama a ho. I didn't get why they called me White girl. My dad had organized postal workers to go to the 1965 March on Washington; before that I didn't know differences existed among

Blacks. We were all in the same ship together, he told me. I believed that being Black, a name I called myself even though some people still used "Negro," was something we shared, like having the same last name. To say I wasn't Black made no sense to me.

My mother never could understand why I would come home in tears every day after school. Her response was ignore them, "they're just jealous." It meant nothing to me. In my eyes I was the odd man out and I only wanted to be in, to be like everybody else in school, to trade my Stride Rite oxblood oxfords for white go-go boots from Baker's. I realized, at twelve, that I was on my own. My mother's idea of an antidote was to put me with girls who, in her eyes, were like me. I tried to be a good sport for my mother, but most of her ideas made me restless. In Brownies, making pot holders and earning patches was about as interesting to me as watching grass grow. The idea of moving up to Girl Scouts caused night sweats. I didn't want to hurt my mother by telling her how I felt; instead, one day at a Brownie meeting I mixed a wad of gum with glue and put it on my Brownie leader's chair. The class went wild when she sat down and got up with the chair stuck to her butt. She knew I had done it because everybody was laughing and looking at me. The trouble I got into when I got home was worth it, though, because I was freed from moving up to Girl Scouts. My mother had moved on to the idea that I needed to know about art—"culture" was the word she used. She enrolled me in Saturday art appreciation classes at the Newark Museum. She got me up early, dressed me, and took me downtown to sit on the marble floor and listen to some bored Livingston housewife ramble on about long-dead artists and their strokes, techniques, and muses. The teacher was patronizing to Evelyn Hawkins, Eddie Hauser, and me, the only brown ones in the bunch. Eddie's mother was Black and his father was Jewish. Whenever one of us asked a question she would usually tell us that there were things she didn't expect us to understand. I began to despise the woman's pale, pinched face encased in a mass of blond straw. I took my frustration out on Evelyn, the class brown-noser. One day, when we were painting abstracts, I dumped my water bucket onto Evelyn's head. My mother stopped making me go. I was left with dance and piano.

I learned to straddle. At home with my neighborhood friends, they accepted me as a member of the tribe, no questions asked. At school, I had to watch everything I said so I wouldn't have to fight. But the line of girls wanting to fight me continued to grow. My mother was nonplussed when I would come home crying every day. "Just knock one of 'em out and the rest of them will leave you alone," she'd say. Looking at my peach-sized fist, I couldn't imagine it had the power to render one unconscious, but I vowed to fight back the next time I was picked on. JoAnn Durwell and her two older sisters had moved to my neighborhood from the Central Ward projects. They were tough and had the deep cut marks on their faces to prove it. JoAnn and I were in Mr. Walker's seventh-grade class and she'd begun sending me threatening notes that read simply "Outside" or "You and me, after school" early in the school year. I lived with a dry mouth and a rapid heartbeat. One day in spring when the class was cutting and putting up construction-paper flowers, raindrops, and water cans, JoAnn came up from behind me where I was sitting in the center of the room and punched me in my back. I dropped the scissors that I'd been using and walked to the back of the class, where she had run. She was laughing at me. I walked right up to her and punched her, with all my strength, on the side of her nose. She paused for a moment and then came at me, arms swinging like a windmill. I went toward her, my arms blocking and punching. I was a mad dog and proceeded to wipe the floor with her. Mr. Walker, who had left us alone for a moment to get glue from the art room, rushed to the back of the class, where everyone was cheering from atop desks and chairs. He pulled us apart, with each of us accusing the other of starting it. He walked us to the principal's office, where we had to sit, facing each other, as we waited for our mothers to come. She looked at me. I looked at the floor. I felt relieved that it was all over, believing, as my mother had told me, that if I beat one of them up, the rest would leave me alone. I wanted to feel that the dread that I had lived with over the last year was over. My mother came and got me. On the way home, I talked so fast, trying to tell her, blow by blow, what had happened, that I kept running out of breath. She was glad that I'd fought back and once again assured me that the rest of the toughs would now leave me alone. The next day when I got to school, I sat down at my desk and found a note written on a piece of loose-leaf paper on my desk. It was from another girl, from a different class. It read: "Today, me and you, after school."

By the time I got to high school, I'd decided that it was easier to just be who people thought I was. I joined a sorority of obnoxious girls who hung in a pack, wore the latest fads, and specialized in making kids with less material things feel bad. I became part of the group who intimidated by seeming superior. It was the beginning of my death.

I CHECKED MY REflection in the mother-of-pearl compact Miles had given me several years earlier when we were a couple. A pretty woman looked back at me, and I acknowledged her, even with the clumping mascara and the pores that were drinking my foundation. I snapped the compact shut and dropped it into my suede shoulder sack.

"You look good," Cheryl said as she shifted her Scirocco into second, then first gear, swooping into the curb in front of the Delta entrance.

"I need some powder."

"Your skin looks fine."

"I need something."

"Yeah, a lobotomy."

"Thanks."

We laughed and leaned over to hug.

"Call me when you get home."

"First thing. I had a great time."

"Me too. I'm so glad you came down."

We hugged again and pressed our tear-streaked cheeks together. It was always hard to say good-bye, and this visit had been especially emotional.

Cheryl held the seat so I could grab my overstuffed Coach duffel. I looked at my Movado and tried to calculate how long it would take me to find an ATM. I knew I was pushing it, but I had to get twenty dollars to pay for the cab ride home. I didn't want to rely on finding a full ATM on a Sunday night at La Guardia. Cheryl and I had spent all of our cash eating out, shopping, and going to movies during my five-day visit. We needed to treat ourselves 'cause she had just been dumped by her boyfriend, the one she'd moved to Atlanta for, the one she'd put through law school. Coming back from a self-induced coma was hard work. I also hadn't dated anyone since Miles and was a little lonely.

I noticed a brother in a velvety-looking chocolate leather jacket, emptying his pockets to go through the security gate again. Great, I thought as I walked to the gate behind him, prepared to be pissed because I was close to missing my flight and still had to find a cash machine. I bumped his onion-shaped behind, which was nicely settled in a pair of Levi's 501 jeans, with my duffel. He wore a Red Sox cap and had large dark curls peeking from underneath.

"Oh, I'm sorry," I said, clearly making a bigger deal out of tapping him than it was.

He turned around, and I wanted to gasp. His golden skin seemed candlelit. His dark lush lashes were enough for me to pack up and move to wherever he lived.

"No problem," he said, smiling at me and revealing a set of teeth that had to have been helped by braces.

Of course, I reasoned, his cap could be concealing a bald head, but he was so fine, it wouldn't have mattered. He walked through, grabbed his caramel-colored Dunhill from the conveyor belt, and walked toward his gate.

After I found a cash machine and secured twenty of the fifty dollars left in my account, I headed toward my flight, calculating how I was going to live until I got paid, four days from now. With five minutes to get to my gate, I began running.

"Catch your breath, girl," a pleasant-looking Black male reservationist said to me as I panted and waved my ticket before him.

"I had to find—a—cash—"

"I know. It's just ridiculous there's not one here."

"Did I miss it?" I asked, looking at an ajar jetway door.

"No. It's still here. The flight's basically empty. I can even bump you up to first class," he said, pausing to purse his Vaseline-coated lips. "That is, if you like?"

"I'd love. I really need a comfortable ride home, and some champagne would be really nice. Thank you."

"No problem, girl. Whenever I can help one of us, you know, I do, 'cause that's what it's about," he said, the last part in a conspiratorial whisper that made me want to laugh.

"Well, thank you"—I looked at his nameplate—"Darryl Rogers. I really appreciate it."

"You're welcome, Miss Andrews, and you have a nice flight."

It was one of those times when being Black helped.

I glanced at my boarding pass as I made my way down the jet

way: 3A. I had traveled in first class only one other time, when Miles and I went to Paris two years ago. Holding it with both hands, I steered my overpacked duffel onto the plane and a few feet to my seat in the third row. I saw that my seat mate was holding a *Wall Street Journal* in front of his face, the body language loudly saying, "Don't talk to me." I saw the Red Sox cap and thought, There is a God.

"Excuse me, please—"

"Oh, hi. Here, let me help you with that," he said, getting out of his seat to put my duffel in the overhead.

I moved past the crumpled newspaper that was on his seat and settled into the window seat. How could I have been this lucky? I thought, watching his gray T-shirt struggle to get free from its tucked Levi's position as he reached into the overhead luggage compartment. Confident men who seemed too good to be true were my weakness. I love men in Levi's. Not Lee, too boxy. Not Wrangler, too Bama. Levi's were my favorite, right up there with British sports cars and baseball caps.

"I'm Jack," he said, settling back in his seat and extending his hand.

"Hi, I'm Alice, the clumsy one."

He laughed. "And a sense of humor, too," he said, and flashed that Ultra Brite smile again.

Calm down, I told myself. I was a different person now. I was working on the interiors, although I was glad that I'd listened to Cheryl and done my hair and makeup. Cheryl believed in hair and makeup. "It's the finish every woman needs," was her mantra. I liked the way I looked without makeup but recognized a huge difference when I put some on. My skin tone, a deep medium brown, was boring, and foundation made it more interesting, "Burnt

Pecan," just like the bottle promised. My thick, medium-length hair was no longer bone straight but gently relaxed, which gave it a full, often wild look when I wore it loose, which wasn't that often. It was just so much easier to wear it pulled up or back.

I looked down at Jack's bare, practically hairless forearm propped on the wide first-class armrest and made a mental note that I was several tones deeper than he. Probably likes women who look more "other" than Black, I decided, and concluded that I wasn't his type. Upper-class Black men, the kind I figured him to be based on his perfect teeth, conservative watch—Baume & Mercier or Cartier—and tight diction, went wild for Black women with racial backgrounds that were at half-mast.

"So, you from New York?" he asked.

"Sort of. I live in Manhattan now, but I'm from New Jersey."

"Oh, yeah, where?"

I hated this question, particularly so soon in conversation. I knew that most people thought of Newark as the armpit of the country, overrun with an impoverished population of drug addicts and welfare cheats. Ever since my first year in college, I had become defensive about it. I'd recently read a memoir by Grace Mirabella, the former editor-in-chief of *Vogue,* who was also from Newark. I could have written it myself:

> For people in Manhattan, where I've spent my entire adult life, New Jersey is more than a place; it's an adjective, and what it describes is just about anything Manhattanites find aesthetically or morally undesirable. . . . The fact of my being from New Jersey has at times been taken to have a certain charm, but the fact of my being from Newark is generally viewed as so unconscionable that most people who have written about me at various points in my

career have literally struck it from the record. According to them, I was born either in South Orange or Maplewood, towns where I did live or go to school at some point in my life, and I've never seen fit to correct them. For I've seen the dangerous effect that "New Jersey" can have on unsuspecting people. New York socialite Marietta Tree, for one, nearly dropped dead when she first heard I was from the Garden State.

My Black Mount Holyoke classmates from New Jersey were from places like Teaneck, South Orange, or Montclair. To them I was an aberration. From my White classmates, I constantly heard, "You don't seem like you're from Newark," which meant "How could someone who seems so refined be from a place so unrefined?" If Jack said it, I'd be forced to dismiss him as a possible.

I felt protective of my hometown, the way a person is of an old dog who looks shabby to strangers but is adorable to its owner. Of course Newark had many problems, but there were still some good things about it, like the Weequahic section, where I grew up; the new museum and sculpture garden; the Ballantine Mansion; parts of the North Ward with its glorious Italianate mansions near Branch Brook Park, which had more cherry blossoms than Washington, D.C.; and, mostly, the people. I opted to resist showing my defensiveness to Jack.

"I'm from Newark."

"Oh, yeah? I have relatives in Montclair."

Of course you do, I thought divisively. "So where are you from?" I asked tentatively, hoping to uncover some personal data that would contradict the negative opinion I was forming.

"Boston and New York. I lived in Massachusetts till I was fourteen, then we moved to Harlem."

Hmmm, Harlem. Maybe he wasn't an elitist, I thought.

•

He leaned back in his seat, took off his baseball cap, and ran his fingers through his large black curls. And he wasn't bald.

"Yup, Harlem, USA. A Hundred Thirty-eighth."

Striver's Row. Old Black money, probably.

"Some beautiful brownstones there," I said.

"Yeah, I lived in a great old house. My mom still lives there."

"Is she alone?"

"Yeah, my dad died a couple years ago."

"Oh, I'm—"

"Yeah. Well, it happens—"

"So where do you live now?" I hastened to change the subject.

"East Side, Eighty-fifth Street."

Who lives on the East Side? Probably is a snob, I thought.

"So, Alice, what do you do?"

"I work for a newspaper in Newark."

"Oh yeah, doing what?"

"Um, I write."

Another thing I hated revealing about myself. I'd discovered that people receive reporters one of two ways. If they're lawyers or government workers, they hate reporters and punctuate their sentences with, "I hope this is off the record," even though you're at a social event doing the electric slide. Then there are the ones, the regular people, who are overly impressed and are eager to know who was the most interesting person you've interviewed.

"So, you're a newspaper reporter?"

"Yep."

"Well, that's really interesting. I've never met a reporter before. What's it like?"

Before I could answer, an attractive Latin-looking crimson-lipped flight attendant came along, offering champagne from a bottle that was wrapped in a white linen towel.

•

I took a sip and closed my eyes, letting the nectar lubricate my thoughts.

"So what do you do?" I asked him.

Jack took a gulp and smiled at me. His intentional three-second pause was the buildup, I knew that. I hated asking that question, but it was what was done in my set. Negro Geography was the only game in town, and either you knew how to play or you got trampled.

"I'm a surgeon. I work at Mount Sinai as an attending."

A surgeon. I maintained my composure. I didn't want to seem overly impressed, but I was. I didn't want him to feel I was too blasé, either.

"An attending? What does that mean?"

"I'm on staff at the hospital, and I perform general surgery as well as teach residents surgery. I didn't think I'd like the teaching part, but I actually enjoy it."

"Better than doing surgery?"

"No, nothing comes close to that."

"Why's that?"

"I don't know. I think it's part power—you know, reaching into someone's body, using your hands to make them better. But, if I were really honest, I'd have to say it's the power of it."

I reflected on Jack's candidness and wondered how the power trip displayed itself in his personal life. He had touched my forearm when making his point, letting his finger linger just a little. I knew something was happening and was already calculating the next step once we were off the plane. I silently cursed the custom of my social milieu that made every unattached, successful male potentially "the one." I could never just meet a guy and get to know him first before planning how his name would sound with mine. I was now trying to train myself to slow down when I met a new man. To get to know him first and to stop looking for the romance novel, sweaty-palm, room-spinning feeling. Maybe I'd try out my new approach on Jack, who seemed like a perfectly suitable kind of guy and who was fine, even though he didn't make my underwear wet the way Miles did.

•

THE MONDAY AFTER I met Jack felt different. The usual dreariness wasn't there. We were having dinner at eight, and I had a hard time focusing at work. All day my heart was beating at hyper pace. I looked around the muted gray-and-beige newsroom and tried to look busy. I picked up the phone to make police checks, routine calls to police precincts to see if anything newsworthy had happened overnight. It was one of the things I hated about my job. All cub reporters were responsible for little towns in each New Jersey county. I would have to call fourteen every day and ask the desk sergeant who answered the phone if anything had happened. They always said no, and I'd say thanks and hang up. I never once got a major story doing police checks. Sometimes I dropped in on them and took a look at the police blotter myself, which went over about as big as a pig at Passover, especially in the towns where someone's prized tomato crop still makes the front page of the local weekly. Fortunately for me, that was only a small part of my job. I liked the feature stuff and usually got to do my ideas.

There must be something wrong with him, I thought between calls. Beautiful, great teeth, intelligent, a doctor. Jack had that well-raised look, good skin and teeth, always a giveaway. The bigger the fish, the bigger the flaw, Cheryl would say. There was probably something big wrong with him, like he had three ex-wives and six kids and all his money went to child support or he was into White girls, although I could usually spot those boys by the way they walked and the way they didn't look you in the eye. Maybe he was bi, one of those boys who never really came out and when AIDS hit jumped back into the closet and turned off the light.

I looked down at the photocopied sheet of police precinct numbers. Just as I attempted to dial another number, Betty, the newsroom secretary, came toward me, beaming, carrying a bouquet of pale yellow cut French tulips that practically covered her entire upper body. I forbade myself to hope that they were from Jack. Betty put them down on my desk and stood in front of me. She wasn't leaving until she found out who had sent them. It didn't matter that she wouldn't know him, Betty just wanted a name and a brief bio. I pulled the envelope from the plastic pitchfork. The card read "To serendipity." I felt warm all over, and then my stomach felt mildly queasy. Betty was staring greedily. She was old enough to be my grandmother and had been working at the paper forever, so she did whatever she wanted.

•

"I met him at the airport. He was on my flight back from Atlanta. He's cute, single, and a doctor," I said by rote.

"A doctor," she exclaimed in her Lower East Side accent. "How nice. Will you see him again?" She knew she was pushing it.

"I'm seeing him tonight. Now, Betty, I've gotta get to work."

She walked away, satisfied, her pink terry-cloth Dearfoams scraping the floor.

Working in a newsroom is a lot like living in a sorority house—everybody feels free to be in your business. Most of the younger reporters were friendly, hung out together after work at a nearby bar for a few drinks before heading home to a dinner of Stouffer's for one. Bob Wojack was new at the paper, came after a few years in book publishing, where he'd decided the pace was not right for him. He was funny and irreverent and hadn't had to work for anything since he was born with a trust fund and a connected family. We were buddies.

"So who's the new boy on the scene?" Bob asked, standing over my desk as I sat hunched over my terminal, trying to write a short about a rash of mysterious fires set in abandoned buildings in Orange.

"Hey, Bob. Busy. Can't talk now," I said.

"Yeah, sure. Just give me the five W's."

"I promise to tell all tomorrow. I've got to be outta here by seven."

"Mmmm. Hot date already? Or was that last night, hence the flowers today?"

"You're such a jerk—"

"Tell me something I don't know."

"Go away, Bob. We can grab lunch tomorrow, okay?"

"Oh, all right, missy."

He bunched up his rep tie and his yellow oxford-cloth shirt in his hand, pretending to be hurt, and walked away. I got back to my piece and was able to send it to my editor's computer and have him look it over and be out of the newsroom in time to make it over the bridge by seven-fifteen. I could dash home for a quick touch-up and be at the restaurant by eight.

I opened the door to my dark rent-stabilized studio, and my black Abyssinian, Essa, was on her usual windowsill perch, watching the traffic on West End Avenue. Her green eyes flashed at me as if to say "I know you're not wearing that, Miss Thing." I had actually considered wearing my work clothes, slim tan wool gab skirt, tan silk shirt, pearls, brown Ferragamos, because the outfit says "I just came from work, and this date is no big deal." But this did mean something, and I decided to just put in the time to reflect that. There was something about him, or was it just me being forever hopeful? Miles had devastated me, had been a really bad choice, and the sex had kept my head cloudy for two years. I had to be brave, even though Jack scared the shit out of me. He could either be a dog, like Miles, or he could be a really nice guy, in which case I'd probably get bored. Either way I was screwed, but I jumped into the shower and redid my makeup anyway. I put on a low-cut white tunic and a long black knit skirt. Understated. Perfect. Aunt Thelma had taught me that. Always better to underdo and always keep the jewelry simple—one great piece or quiet earrings and maybe something at the neck. I grabbed my knit shawl on the way out. I needed something heavier, it was October, but nothing else would look right with the outfit, so I'd just freeze until I jumped into a cab.

Cafe des Artistes is a romantic institution in New York, although I'd never liked it. Its floral banquettes and mirrored walls were a little too burlesque for me, but I was glad he had suggested a place with an intimate kind of reputation. Jack was already there when I got there. I was glad I was only a few minutes late because the maître d' wouldn't seat him until the entire party was there. Jack and I did a polite face touch.

"Mmm," he said when he got a whiff of my Annick Goutal. "You smell good."

"Do you like it?" I said.

"Yeah. It's really different, not perfumy."

The busboy overfilled my glass, and Jack gave him a stern look.

"It's just this stuff I picked up. I never tell what I'm wearing," I said, moving into the banquette. "I did that once, and the woman, she was this woman at my office, went out and got it. It drove me crazy every time I walked by her desk because she would pour on too much, and soon I couldn't stand the smell of it."

"Ah, so there's a method."

"Usually."

We both laughed nervously.

"Well, you can rest assured I'm not gonna go out and buy it."

"Well, thank you."

"And you look beautiful. I like that. What's that top called?"

"It's a tunic."

"Really nice."

"Thank you. Oh, and thank you for the flowers. They're just beautiful."

"Oh, good, you got them. Good, I'm glad you liked them."

"They're my favorites, but I don't remember telling you that."

"You didn't have to tell me. I just like them; can't I like French tulips?"

"Well, most men don't veer too far from the standard."

"Well, I like to think I'm not like most men."

I reconsidered that he might be bi. Most straight guys went for roses, the sure thing, and if not roses, then they let the florist choose, which ended up being some over-the-top exotic monstrosity. These were elegant and simple.

After a bottle and a half of Chardonnay, seared tuna, and a cappuccino, I was sure he wasn't bi and reasonably certain that he wasn't into White girls. That he was a womanizing hound was still a possibility but too soon to know.

Jack's lashes gave him a trustworthy, boyish look. He was fine, easily the finest man that I'd been out with in a very long time. He had gorgeous soft skin that I wanted to feel next to my body. I wanted to go to bed with him but knew it was way too soon. Big fish must be reeled in slowly, I heard Cheryl say in my head. Plus I didn't want him to think I was a slut. There's a rigid code among the Bup—Black urban professional—crowd. The rule is three dates before any heavy petting and then screw on the fourth or fifth, usually at some weekend bed-and-breakfast in New England if you're on the East Coast, Tahoe or Catalina on the West Coast. You only do it after some structure has been established, like you're exclusive or working on getting there. Do it sooner or without an agreement and you're considered a slut at worst, no pedigree at best. A guy who tries to pressure a woman too soon is usually a low-life or doesn't consider her as serious mate material. Both would be outside of the pool of marriageables. When the relationship moves on to "going to meet the parents" phase and staying overnight, separate bedrooms are a must, even if the parents say they don't mind. The mothers always mind.

"So, Jack, how'd you end up growing up in Boston?"

I wanted him to keep talking, and I was curious about his Boston connection. My experience with Black folks from Boston, the middle-class ones at school, at least, was that they considered themselves different from most other run-of-the-mill Black folk. It wasn't just a matter of being brought up in Boston, I'm talking about the ones who had been there for a while, a few generations. The longer your family had lived there, the better your social standing among the elite or the Talented Tenth.

"Actually it was Brookline. I lived with my grandparents until I was fourteen."

"Why was that?"

"Uh, 'cause my father was doing his residency in the South and going south in those days was like going to Vietnam to my grandparents."

"So they lived in Brookline?"

"Yeah. My grandparents moved there in the late forties, early fifties, from Cambridge."

"And where were they from originally?"

"As far back as we know, Boston. At least since the mid-1880s, they, we, descended from freeborn people of color, who had come from either the Dominican Republic or Haiti."

I took another swig of Chardonnay. I was suddenly starting to feel like the little inferior scholarship kid who faked her social status all through college, telling people my father was a doctor when he was really a mailman. I wanted to know more about Jack and his family, even though I risked feeling worse. Before Holyoke, I didn't even know that there were Black people like him and his family, generations of college-educated folk.

"So what did they do? I mean, what kind of business?"

"You really want to know all this stuff?"

"Yes, I'm really interested."

"Is this your reporter's curiosity?"

"Not completely."

"Well, let's see, my great-grandfather, James, was a tailor; apparently, according to family legend, he made a lot of moneymaking suits for Boston's Brahmins. Shortly after the turn of the century, around 1910, when department stores began opening up with ready-made suits, he was put out of business."

"So then what?"

"Well, by that time my great-grandparents were middle-aged and had money put away. They moved to Cambridge and—"

"And what about your grandparents, the ones you lived with?"

"This is all on the paternal side now, and my grandfather, who was as much my father as my dad, um, became a doctor and set up his practice first in Cambridge and then in the house in Brookline."

"That's really something—I mean, a major accomplishment, especially back then."

"Yeah, I guess so. My grandfather was really some man. He graduated from Harvard in 1926, thirty-six years after W. E. B. Du Bois. There were six Blacks in Du Bois's class, and there were still only ten Black students in Papa's. Those were the kinds of things I grew up hearing, recited around the dinner table."

"Well, sounds like he had a lot to be proud of. Your family, Jack, would make a great story. Has anyone ever approached you about it?"

"Well, yeah, the story has been told in the old days in the old Negro presses, but my grandmother was very modest and didn't like a whole lot of attention or peacocking, as she used to call it."

"Sounds like a whole different world."

"Well, you're a Holyoke girl, I'm sure your background isn't all that different."

Now was my opportunity to tell him, to show him who I really was, let him decide right now, in the beginning, if he wanted to keep going or cut it off. Our backgrounds were different, so what, right? I mean, what was the big deal, anyway? I wished that were true. It was a big deal. I didn't even know my great-grandfather's name, much less what he did for a living or even where he lived. My grandfather was a sharecropper, the other one a farmer. Not exactly part of the Talented Tenth.

"So why'd they move to Brookline?" I needed to uncover something awful about these people, to punch holes, see some rot in what seemed to me a perfect family tree. Maybe they had moved to get away from all the southern darkies who were migrating into Cambridge and the South End section.

"My great-grandfather moved the family to a Cambridge brownstone, when my grandfather Evander was born. I guess it was what their social set was doing at the time."

"And your grandmother, was she from Boston, too?"

"No, she wasn't, and at the time it caused quite the uproar. He met Grandma Ida through a distant cousin. She was from Kansas, also from a family of freeborns, but Kansas is not Boston, and apparently the other families in Boston and in New York, Philadelphia, and D.C., where the rest of their social group lived, were not happy that he'd gone outside the tribe to choose a wife. Everyone wanted to know who was this Ida Singleton the Russworm boy was marrying."

"Tribe?"

"That's what they used to call themselves—"

"Who?"

"The other families in New York and Philly and D.C. who came from freeborns."

"So the Russworms were really something," I said, thinking about Du Bois's phrase, the Talented Tenth, with their fine education and manners, which he said was the top portion of Blacks who should represent the rest of the race.

"I guess so."

"Oh, don't be modest. Am I sitting here with landed gentry?"

"Oh no, far from it."

I could tell he was being modest. "Is your grandfather the reason you became a doctor?"

"Oh, no question. He was my hero."

The sweetness of that made me like him.

"So, Alice, we spent the whole night talking about me, so we'll have to have another date so I can hear the story of your life."

"Well, it's pretty boring, but I'd be happy to tell you all about it," I lied.

"How about Saturday? Some dinner, maybe a movie, something casual?"

"Saturday would be good."

JACK AND I WERE having our second date. I was meeting him in front of the sixplex on the Upper West Side. Outside, the theater was surrounded by its usual Saturday night crowd—new yuppie parents seeing a movie for the first time in six months, quads of women who worked in advertising, and pairings of gay men and fag hags, dressed in immaculate casual clothes and looking like Banana Republic ads.

I watched Jack getting out of a cab, and I was struck, again, by how handsome he was, how well he wore it. Like broken-in cowboy boots. He emitted confidence, and I envied him. He seemed to have never had a day of self-doubt, never had people picking on him. I resented him for how easy his life seemed to have been, for coming from a family where everyone around the table spoke the same language. At one time, I had felt closeness toward my family, but by the time I was ten, that had begun to erode. My brother and I have been estranged since I was ten and he was twelve and he tried to have sex with me, although at the time I didn't know what sex was. Years later, when I was seeing the campus shrink for what was considered general senior malaise, it came up. The incest. I'd never told a soul. Never consciously thought about it, but the leather scent of the shrink's office began prying all my secrets loose. My brother and I had been as close as twins, constantly together and always sharing secrets. We were twenty months apart. One day he came home from school with a strange wild look, wilder than what was normal even for him. Come upstairs. Be quiet. Open your legs. Put them up. Don't ever tell anybody. I wanted to please him. It wouldn't fit. He tried to jam it a few times, and I yelled out, It hurts. After several tries he stopped. Don't ever tell anybody. For years I pushed it down and pretended I was the same little girl, but I never was. I went from being wild and free, a tomboy, to a woman-child obsessed with having a perfect appearance. I was no longer capable of being free. Nothing made me happy. My father, to whom I had been very close, began to disgust me. His routine for forty years has been getting up every day before the sun, eating oatmeal, and wrapping a Spam sandwich in waxed paper to take to work.

Jack seemed so comfortable with life. As though he knew how to handle anything that he'd face, because he wasn't damaged. He'd been prepared. His face was open, like a child's. I had secrets that I clung to because I was ashamed. The school shrink helped me to see that I wouldn't have a successful relationship as long as I held on to these secrets. I had to set them free in order to be free. I told myself I could deal with being honest with Jack about my family and my feelings about my dad working at the post office. Never in forty years did I ever hear my father complain about going to work. Maybe Jack would say that my father was doing the honorable thing, taking care of his family. But what about the incest? It was ugly and undignified and made me feel damaged. I couldn't tell him.

I watched Jack walk toward me. I was leaning on a parking meter, trying to look like a normal, happy person, pushing away my thoughts of that day when I was ten.

"Hi there," I said cheerfully.

"Hey"—he kissed me on the cheek—"you look great."

"Thanks."

I'd bought a new outfit and spent a good part of the day getting ready. Hair, makeup, trying to look casual, but the effect took hours to achieve.

"You been waiting long?"

"Nope, just got here."

"So, this line looks pretty intense."

"Um, yeah, the one we want is sold out."

"Ugh. Well, whaddya wanna do? Get a drink?"

"That sounds great." I needed a drink.

We headed down the block to a quasi-Mexican restaurant so popular with the movie crowd that they didn't have to serve good food or offer reasonable prices. I ordered a margarita and Jack had a gin and tonic.

"So," Jack said after we'd settled into the pine-and-leather booth. "How was your day?"

"Fine. I, um, did some laundry, went to the bookstore—"

"Oh yeah? What'd you get?"

"Oh, this psychobabble thing I'd been wanting to read."

"What?"

"It's called *The Drama of the Gifted Child.*"

"Uh-huh. What's it about?"

"Oh, I don't know, just stuff about your childhood and how you're affected by it."

"Mmm. So, did you have some childhood trauma?"

It was an interesting way of putting it, and I didn't quite know how to answer. Trauma seemed so big a word, as if I'd have to have been a survivor of war or a pawn in a horrible divorce. I was neither, but my childhood pain felt just as large. I realized this was an opportunity to tell him about Lucas, but it was too soon to spill such pain. On the other hand, I could give him a peek at my baggage to give him a chance to run if he couldn't deal.

"Um, well, nothing catastrophic." I let the moment pass.

Jack motioned for the waiter, and I was off the hook. He ordered a second gin and I anxiously ordered another margarita.

"So, Alice, how is your life?" Jack asked, and took a mouthful of ice cubes from his first highball glass.

"You mean—"

"I mean now, what's going on?"

"Well, as I've told you, my career is going okay. Actually, it could be better. I'm starting to feel a little bored with it."

"How long have you been there?"

"Almost four years—"

"And what's the problem?"

"Well, I'm feeling that I'm hitting that glass ceiling." I didn't want to tell him the real deal because I didn't want to seem like a complainer.

"Mmmm. What do you wanna do?"

"I'm not sure what I wanna do for life, but at the paper, I'd like some better assignments, maybe a beat covering national affairs instead of all the metro stuff."

"What's the metro stuff?"

"The stuff you probably don't read, urban violence, features about thirty-year-old grandmothers, city hall graft, and it's assigned to the Black reporters."

"Mmm, I see. Kinda like you're Black, so you're a know about pathology?"

"You got it."

"That is just so insulting, to just assume you know about the ghetto because you're Black."

"Yeah."

"Well, why don't you just tell them that you aren't that kind of Black? I mean, what could you possibly understand of a thirty-year-old grandmother? How can you make sense of that?"

"I know."

"When I was doing my residency at Mass General, I was working in the ER, the emergency room, and this old Black man came in complaining about chest pains. Anyway, this intern was with him, asking questions, trying to determine what was wrong, and the man, the patient, spoke with a heavy sort of southern dialect. The intern was White and from somewhere in the Midwest. Anyway, he came looking for me, now I'm the chief resident, because he couldn't understand what the old man was saying and wanted me to translate. This kid just assumed that I would understand the guy because we were both Black."

"Hmmm, what did you do?"

"I asked him about his background, his parents' profession and such, and just as I figured, the intern was merely second-generation college educated. I let him know right then and there that he was closer to that patient's background than I. It's maddening, but what're ya gonna do? I don't let it get to me."

I sat listening, in awe of Jack's indignation. I was beginning to feel like he'd shown me a side I didn't want to see. His superiority was a little offputting, but he was clueless and just went on.

"It enrages me, but I just look at that kind of stuff as their problem. It's their limitations, not mine."

"Well, that's a much healthier attitude," I said.

"Yeah, my grandfather taught me that."

Things were moving along. Jack had called me every night since our first date last Monday. We'd talked about our days, our friends, a little more about our families. I'd told him some bits about past relationships. Neither of us was seeing anyone else seriously. I wasn't seeing anyone at all, but I assumed, if he was like most men, that he had a few women he dated. I wanted to like him and tried to cover over the stain he'd just shown me.

"You talk about your grandfather all the time—"

"Yeah, well, he was my hero. He taught me a lot."

"What's the biggest thing?"

"That's a good question. Um, let's see, he taught me not to ever settle—"

"Mmm. Is that why you're still single?"

"Whoa, now there's a reporter ambush." Jack laughed and I smiled.

"I didn't mean—"

"No, it's okay. It's another good question. You're very perceptive, Alice. I like that."

"Thanks." I didn't know what else to say.

"I like you. You're direct but not hard. Um, I don't know why I'm single. Why aren't you married?"

•

"Oh, I guess I just haven't found the right fit."

"What are you looking for?"

"I don't know, somebody who understands me, I guess."

"Is that hard?"

"I don't think so."

He paused and looked down at his drink. "I almost got married once," he said, trying to sound nonchalant.

"Really?"

"Yeah. We broke up about four years ago."

"What happened? I mean, I don't want to pry."

"Pry. It's all right."

"So what happened?"

Jack looked at his watch. We'd been sitting for a little over an hour. It was occurring to both of us that this conversation was going to usurp the movie.

"You wanna order dinner?" he asked.

"Sure."

"Good. I didn't really want to see a movie anyway. I like talking to you."

"Yeah. Me too. So?"

"So. Let's see, um. I met her up in Boston, when I was doing my residency. She was a senior at Wellesley and we were at this party in Roxbury. Sherry Steptoe. You don't know her, do you?"

"No—I would remember that name."

"Good. Well, Sherry and I were going to be the perfect match. We came from the same background, knew the same people—"

"So what happened, from the beginning?"

"You really want to hear this?"

"Yeah, I really do."

"Okay, well, let's see. She walked into this party and I saw her. It was winter and she was wearing this beret. When she took it off, her hair had all this static electricity. Her hair was long and thick and kind of reddish brown. I walked up to her and said, 'I know this sounds like a line, but haven't I seen you before?' I really thought that I had. She looked me up and down, which for her wasn't hard because she's almost six feet. I'm only six two. After literally sizing me up, she said, 'Maybe, who do you know here?' I looked around the room. The crowd was all these well-scrubbed recent professional school graduates. I told her that I knew Ken and Iris. Iris is Sherry's cousin, and she, Iris, was giving the party for Ken, her boyfriend who had just graduated from Harvard Law, made *Law Review,* and was going to work for Willkie Farr or one of those gigantic firms here."

A waiter dressed in a rough dried violet cotton shirt came to take our order. I asked for the grilled salmon, and Jack ordered the grilled chicken breast. I felt happy, or maybe it was just my third margarita.

"So, where was I?" Jack seemed to revel in telling this story.

"Um, you asked her if you'd met before, she looked you up and down, and you looked around—"

"Oh, uh-huh. So I introduced myself, just giving my first name, and I extended my hand. Now, I knew I was breaking the code among the tribe by not giving her my last name, but I was tired. It was the end of the month and I had been on call and just wasn't up for the game. Also, I was just testing her, to see if she'd talk to me without knowing my pedigree. But she did exactly as I thought she would. She became impatient and said, 'Jack what? You do have a last name, don't you?' I complied, I'm ashamed to say, and told her my last name, which I knew in the crowd we were in in Boston, most people knew."

"So, we're talking about the tribe again?" I asked, even though I didn't need edification.

"Yeah, pretty much everybody there was from an old Black Boston family. I gave her my whole name—Jack Evander Clayton Russworm, knowing that she'd be impressed. Again, Alice, I'm not proud of this behavior. Sherry recognized the last name and asked what I did. I knew this was just a formality because she had acknowledged that she knew the name and anybody who knew us knew that we were a family of doctors. Her cousin Iris and I had grown up on the Vineyard together. Her mother and my father knew each other from when they were kids. Anyway, the whole scene was as familiar as my own hands. Our parents or grandparents had gone to Howard, Fisk, or AU together. We were all in *Jack and Jill.*"

I imagined the scene. All the women were attractive and expensively dressed in subtle colors. Their skin colors ranged from the whitest to a deep tan or olive. They all wore their hair straight. The guys all had major résumés and were from places like Harvard, Wharton, Stanford, Chicago.

"I have to tell you—remember now, this is five years ago—I wanted to cut out as soon as possible and get Sherry to leave with me. I knew I had to give up the basic bio stuff so she could leave feeling like she wasn't going home with some strange dude.

"I told her that I was doing my surgery residency at Mass. To which she offered that her father was an OB. I knew that he was something, doctor, lawyer, Indian chief, because she was a BAP poster girl," Jack said.

"What do you mean? How could you tell?"

"Um, I can always tell—the way she was dressed, her comportment. You know, the neat, simple black cocktail dress, real pearls, shoulder-length hair bouncin', just a whiff of perfume. Like you."

"I see. So she wasn't dripping in Giorgio?" I added, uneasy with his characterization of me.

•

Jack laughed and continued. "Right, right. So anyway, she left the party with me. We got to my place, and that was it. We just started going out from there, and after a year, we got engaged."

"So why didn't you go through with it?"

"For starters, I didn't love her. It would've been perfect, except for that. She would've been a dutiful wife and mother and a perfect hostess, but that's not what I want."

"When did you figure that out?"

"Unfortunately not until after I gave her the ring. The day after, she was on the phone with hotels and caterers and dressmakers, determined to have a proper June wedding."

"So, what's wrong with that?"

"Nothing in itself, but during all the planning I got to know her and her family, and I didn't like what I saw. Don't misunderstand. I mean, her folks are nice people, they're just a little too caught up in Who's Who in Black Bourgeoisie, going to the Vineyard in the summer, and trying to outbuy each other up there; it was all so predictable. I was headed for a life that was exactly what Papa had warned me against. My grandfather listened to his own beat. He married Grandma Ida, whom no one in his group approved of or understood."

"Why's that?"

"She was a feminist, long before there was the word. She was a social worker at the Y, which in itself was revolutionary; none of Papa's colleagues had wives who worked. What most doctor's wives did back then was start exclusionary colored women's clubs."

"But wasn't she from the same background?"

"She wasn't a member of the tribe, remember, she was from the Midwest, and Grandma Ida didn't straighten her hair, and it wasn't even good hair, either."

Oh, God, I felt a stab in my stomach. He'd said the dread phrase, "good hair." He'd actually said it. I didn't know what to do. Should I tell him, teach him, how wrong such a comment, such thinking, was?

"What do you mean, good hair?"

"Oh, you know, straight hair. I mean what old folks used to call good hair. I don't think of it that way."

"Mmmm. Didn't you tell me that your grandparents had a house on Martha's Vineyard?"

"Yeah, they did, and we still have it, but they didn't go around trying to make it this exclusive thing. A lot of those folks will only associate with you if you've been going for generations. There's all kinds of caste systems within the group that I can't deal with."

"I see. So how'd you actually break up with her?"

"Well, it was the day before—"

"You broke up with her the day before the wedding?"

"Yeah, I know, it was terrible. I couldn't sleep for a week before. At first I just thought it was nerves and it would pass, but when it didn't I knew I had to do something. So I got in the car and drove from Boston to Stamford, that's where her family lives, and called her when I got to the center of town. I remember the phone rang for like ten times before somebody answered it. All the while I was, um, my mouth was dry, my stomach was in knots. When someone finally answered the phone, I could hear a lot of laughing and talking in the background. Now all of her cousins and aunts were there from all over the country. Iris, the cousin I knew, actually answered the phone. I made small talk, knowing it would probably be the last time I talked to her. Once Sherry got on the phone I asked her to meet me in town, at a coffee shop."

"She must've known something was wrong—"

"Oh, yeah, she pressed me, she sensed something, but I just told her to meet me."

•

"And she did?"

"Yeah, she did."

"What was it like waiting for her to show up?"

"Miserable, but I kept telling myself that she'd be okay. She was pretty and smart; she'd just graduated with honors and was starting a new job. I knew she'd easily find someone else."

"Ugh."

"Um, so she showed up and—"

"I can't imagine. What, ah, what do you tell your family, your friends?"

"We agreed that she'd just tell them that she ended it—"

"Have you seen her since?"

"Nope, never saw her again."

"Gosh, Jack. That's some story."

"I know, but I don't regret it. It was the right thing."

I smiled at him, but that good hair slip was still ringing in my ears.

•

5

I HAD FINALLY trained myself to listen to myself. If something about a new guy didn't feel right, now I'd cut it off early on. His "good hair" comment notwithstanding, Jack felt right. I wasn't always like this. So many of my relationships ended badly and abruptly because my choices were bad, because my bags were so heavy. It didn't really begin to dawn on me to listen to my gut until I hit misery, big time. With Miles. The thing with Lucas, which probably caused some of my feelings of outsiderness, and then my efforts to be someone else, had taught me to tune out my own voice, my gut. Now, a little more than a year later, I look back at my relationship with Miles and it's as clear as glass that it was never going to work. He had given me plenty of clues early on, I just chose not to notice.

Our trip to Paris had been a disaster. I wanted to drink café au lait outdoors and Miles wanted to shop. I wanted to take the metro and explore different neighborhoods. He wanted to do the Louvre, not because he was an art lover, but just to say he had been there. But those were small things.

Miles was going to be my Ward Cleaver. I was his BAP, whether I wanted to be one or not. Miles believed that Black women came in three categories: the commoner, the BAP, and the Afrotique. Commoners were women with names like LaQwanda, who wore Lycra regardless of dress size, colored contacts, and two-inch acrylic nails. Their usual form of conversation was telling somebody off with neck gyrating like some rear car ornament from the '70s. Miles had grown up with commoners but had traveled far from home. At the University of Chicago and business school at Harvard, he'd met the other types: BAPs—Black American princesses—and Afrotiques, righteous womanist sisters with natural hair and clothes made from African fabric. In fact, his best friend, Brenda, was an Afrotique. She was his spiritual companion, but her lack of sophistication in expensive equipment disqualified her as girlfriend material. BAPs, with their divine deportment and punctilious preoccupation with things, were more attractive.

Several of my Holyoke classmates whom I hung out with were real BAPs, and I'd adopted many of their rituals: early Saturday morning standing appointments for hair processing, then nails and toes done at one of the zillion Korean nail joints, shopping—always retail—and never riding the subway. Shopping retail and not riding the subway were things I couldn't bring myself to do. My

•

pals, who wouldn't be caught dead on the subway or buying discount at Loehmann's, thought I was just eccentric.

No room for such with Miles. The beginning of the end came one night when he asked me to meet him for a drink at Simone's, a place where, on any given night, Buppies, Block Boys, and pseudo-bohemians are plastered to the glass-and-granite walls like bees in a honeycomb. Miles had asked me to meet him there for a drink after work. He was trying to decide what to do with me by having his friend Brenda size me up, but at the time I didn't want to know that. I just happily went to meet him, even though I detested the place.

I was patiently swirling a goblet of Chardonnay for close to half an hour when Miles came charging toward me.

"Hey, sorry I'm late."

I smiled at him. He was always late.

"What you drinking?" he said, and waved the waiter over. "You'll never guess who I ran into on my way up here."

He said, not waiting for my response, "Brenda, my girl from undergrad."

Actually Brenda had gone to Roosevelt, a much less competitive commuter school not far from the University of Chicago.

"Really?" I said, trying to sound enthusiastic.

"You mind if she joins us?"

"No—of course, I'd like to meet her."

"I'll be right back."

While he was gone getting Brenda, I mentally reviewed what I was wearing: a black turtleneck with a black-and-white houndstooth jacket and trousers, hair pulled up, and a small amount of face powder and red lipstick. I approved. I wasn't done done. I wanted it to be clear to Brenda that I was not one of his bimbos, but someone he was serious about, someone whom he took to client dinners and Paris.

"Alice, this is Brenda. Brenda, this is Alice," Miles said, holding Brenda by the elbow.

I looked up at Brenda and from my seat could see she was short. Her coffee brown skin and tiny locks framed a small, unhappy face.

"Brenda, I finally get to meet you."

Brenda smiled but bared no teeth. Miles pulled out a seat for her and sat down.

"It's nice to meet you, too, I was beginning to think you were Miles's imaginary friend," Brenda said.

She and Miles laughed. I lifted my glass to my lips. Miles reached for his tie and moved the knot.

"Yes, he likes to keep me hidden," I said.

"Naw, baby, you know it ain't like that," Miles said.

"So you work at a women's shelter, Miles says?" I said.

"Yeah, I can't imagine work that's more satisfying."

"What do you do there?"

"Um, it's like what don't I do, you know, not-for-profit work is—"

Before Brenda could finish explaining the unstructured nature of nonprofit agencies, a voice from my past bellowed by our table.

"Alice Andrews, is that you? Is that my homegirl?"

It was Jerome Johnson, bearing a smile that displayed four gold teeth.

"Jerome, how ya doin'? It's great to see you." I smiled and offered Jerome my cheek.

Miles and Brenda looked at each other and then looked at me. I introduced them to Jerome, who was a high school buddy, homeboy turned record producer.

"Whazzup?" he said to them. His latest rap posse standing behind him nodded at us. After a brief exchange consisting of whom from the neighborhood we'd each seen last, Jerome shoved off.

"Nice meetin' y'all," he said to Miles and Brenda. "You take care, girl. You lookin' good, baby," he said to me.

"So, who was that?" Miles said in his best lockjaw, spitting out the "that."

"Oh, a guy I know from my old neighborhood."

"How?" he pressed.

"I don't know, he lived down the street or something."

"Did he go to school with you?"

"Um, maybe elementary school."

"Oh, I was wondering. I mean, he doesn't seem like the day school type."

"Day school?" Brenda asked.

"Yeah, Alice went to one of them fancy private schools."

"Oh, really," Brenda said.

I nodded.

We had a second round before Miles announced, as he always did, that he had to get back to work.

I couldn't wait to get home and call Cheryl for a recap of the evening.

"So what was she like?" Cheryl asked, pushing the mute button to silence Letterman.

"Well, she was short and cute, and at first I felt a little uncomfortable around her."

"Why?"

"'Cause, you know, she's like got locks and she works for a women's shelter."

"So, she's a social worker?"

"Yeah."

"Uh-huh, so you felt like—"

•

"You know. She's like for the people, doing good, not making any money."

"And she was sizing you up?"

"I think. Miles claims he just ran into her—"

"Puhleeze."

"Okay, so he invited her."

"So how do you think you scored?" Cheryl asked scornfully.

"She hated me, and you'll never guess what else happened."

"What?"

"You'll never guess who we ran into at Simone's."

"Who?"

"Jerome Johnson."

"No! From high school?"

"The one."

"How'd he look? I saw him in like *Ebony* or *Jet*—"

"*Black Enterprise,* yeah, he's a record producer. He has gold teeth."

"No!"

"Four of 'um."

"Get outta here. Oh, God! Did he come over to the table?"

"You know it. All loud, with his pants hanging off his butt."

"What'd you do? You didn't play him off?"

"No, no, you know I wouldn't do that."

"Your people, your people. So how did Mr. Miles take Jerome?"

"He sat there looking like he was smelling shit while Jerome was talking, then, after he left, pressed me about how I knew him."

"I wish I could've been a fly on the wall. Mr. Lord Miles and Jerome Johnson together. You know what I say you ought to do with that Miles fool."

"Easier said than done."

•

"I know, honey, but I mean, you and Miles—he doesn't even know you."

"Yeah, yeah, you're right, but why should that matter? He is fabulous."

"Yeah, fabulously awful."

"I know you're right, but I don't know how to tell him the truth now."

"Just start with, you know, I didn't go to Harbor Hollow School of the Great Divine, and Daddy delivers mail, not babies—"

"I know you're right, but you know Miles has a very narrow view of women—"

"Yeah, I know, his stupid categories. Well, doll face, we don't fit into any of them, and that's Miles's stupidity, not yours."

"I know, but—"

"But nothing, you need to tell him. How're you going to marry somebody who doesn't even know who you really are?"

"I know. I'm depressed. I'm going to sleep now."

"All right, girlfriend, but sleep on what I said."

Two weeks after Simone's, I was headed home in a cab after having drinks with a friend, one of the fronters from the "married well" set. The cab was stopped behind a line of cars waiting at a light. We sat idling in front of a hip-hop club, Royce's. I closed my eyes, the Pakistani driver's car cologne and the three glasses of merlot giving me a rush. I had already asked the driver to turn down his music, which sounded to me like a bunch of cardinals on LSD. I couldn't also ask him to throw out his cologne. I looked out of the window, looking for a distraction, and I saw someone who looked an awful lot like Miles coming out of Royce's with a woman dressed in a citron-colored spandex dress, white pumps, and hair or a weave down to her butt. My eyes followed them as they headed toward the red Porsche Carrera parked a few feet from the entrance. He put the key into the lock. I turned away from the window and faced the Plexiglas separating me from the driver. I wanted to ask him to turn the drug-hazed cardinals back on. I needed something, anything, to tune out the noise in my head. One tear began to fall, another one caught up. By the time I got to the Upper West Side, my face was moist. I overpaid the driver and got out.

"Dank you, lady," I heard the driver say before he sped off. I ran upstairs to my apartment and called Miles before I took off my coat. He wasn't at his office and he wasn't at home.

I sat on my sofa bed, still wearing my coat, trying to make sense of what I'd just seen. I thought of a line I'd read somewhere: Coincidence is God's way of remaining anonymous.

•

I WAS BEGINNING to wonder whether my newly valued radar would know how to detect Jack. He was as different as caviar and cupcakes from the men I'd loved.

The first was Abdul. The Nation of Islam was big in Newark when I was growing up. During the late sixties and early seventies it was a major force, especially in places like Harlem, Newark, Detroit, Chicago, and Philadelphia. It was a time that most closely resembled Reconstruction, pre–Jim Crow days, when Blacks were a dominant entrepreneurial force. In Newark, along Bergen Street and South Orange Avenue, two main thoroughfares, the Nation's fish markets, bakeries, Steak 'n Takes, banks, and schools dotted the landscape. The men were really proper, addressing women as "ma'am" or "sister," men were "brother" or "sir." And they were always ammonia clean. The women wore long-flowing pastel-colored skirts and tunics with matching fabric covering their heads that flowed behind them. They didn't speak to nonbelievers, or lost/founds, as the masses were called. There was a movement happening, but most of us lost/founds didn't have a clue. All we really knew about Muslims was that they didn't eat pork and didn't like White people, or devils, as they were called. The ideas the brothers were preaching as they sold their weekly newspaper, *Muhammad Speaks,* while they seemed as foreign as Saturn, weren't really that radical when you went to the temple, their place of worship. They were trying to teach Black people to love themselves—their skin, their hair, each other—to do for self and not to wait for the White man, aka the government, to do for you; to respect yourself. The words were meant to free. Most of this went over the average teenager's head, but my crowd and I thought of ourselves as above average teenagers, we were sophisticated in every sense, so many of us started listening to the brothers selling *Muhammad Speaks* and began finding attractive those close haircuts and bow ties.

I used to go to the Steak 'n Take in my neighborhood at least twice a week to buy a steak sandwich. They were different from the Four Leaf or Tiffany's, the two Black-owned greasy spoons in the neighborhood, where their idea of special service was to ask, "What you want, baby?" Greasy spoons earned their moniker because of the level of cleanliness, I'm sure.

One day at the Steak 'n Take, I paid for my sandwich but left it on the counter. I was halfway home before I realized that I'd left it.

When I went back Abdul, the owner, was standing at the counter, holding the bag for me. All the brothers who worked there were solicitous, and it was hard to know when they were flirting or just being nice. In hindsight, they were flirting.

"*As-salaam-a-lakium,* my sister. How are you today? Looking very beautiful," he said, holding up the aluminum foil–wrapped sandwich that was now in a brown bag.

"F-i-n-e," I drawled. Even though I knew the proper response, I felt silly using the Muslim greeting since I was a nonbeliever. "I forgot my sandwich."

"Yes, sister, I see that. Here you are."

He handed me the bag and held my hand a minute too long. I had noticed him before, but I knew he was a bit older than me and probably married; most of the brothers were married with many children. Be fruitful and multiply. They took it literally. After a few months of prolonged glances and small talk, Abdul asked me out. I was seventeen, he was twenty-seven. A real grown man. He wore suits and drove a Sedan de Ville, like my uncle Dave. He also had three boys and a wife. He was dangerous, and at seventeen, that was just what I wanted.

Until this point in my life, everything had been predictable. I did well in school and most of the other things my mother wanted me to do. Now it was time for me to do something that I wanted to do—flirting quickly, moving to seeing each other. He would pick me up at school and we'd go to eat at hotel restaurants and to a room upstairs. I was a virgin and he was gentle. He used a rubber. I never asked him what he told his wife. I never thought about her, so she didn't exist in my seventeen-year-old mind. I was used to getting what I wanted, and after a few months, I wanted him. He was sure of himself, which was something none of the goofy teenage boys I knew were. He was self-made, and while he wasn't really handsome, once I fell for him he looked like a god. He was the color of brewed coffee, about five feet nine, with broad shoulders and prominent cheekbones. With him, I felt more beautiful than ever because he talked about the looks people couldn't see. He talked about my inner strength and my mind and taught me to play chess. He taught me to think differently.

We carried on for six months before everyone at my high school and his restaurant knew. Then he started talking about leaving his wife. I wanted him to leave her and marry me. I wanted to have his children and wear beautiful long dresses and cook pork-free meals for him, even though I didn't know how to cook.

"My wife knows about you," he announced casually one day when we were in the car driving to Philadelphia to see a movie. "One of the sisters at the restaurant told her and she confronted me and I told her the truth."

I didn't know what to say. It was the first time he'd ever mentioned his wife, and he was so calm. I realized I was in way over my head. These were adult problems, and I was still trying to decide between Mount Holyoke and Oberlin, but I liked the idea of being involved in a real adult drama. I turned in my seat to face him. My behind felt as though it slid on the leather seat.

"So what did she say?"

"She wanted to know about you. She asked me a lot of questions and she wanted to know if I was in love," he said, turning to glance at me.

"And?"

"And I told her I was. I can't lie, Alliyah," he said, using the Arabic name he called me.

"Well, so, now what? Did she throw you out?"

He laughed at me. I smiled, but I didn't understand what was funny.

•

"No, no, love. Muslim women don't throw their husbands out. She was calm and reasonable. I told her that we'd discuss it in a few days."

"What! You told her that and she just said okay? Well, I hope you know that that wouldn't have been my response." I turned back to face the windshield.

"Yes, Alliyah, I do understand that, but in time you will learn."

Now here I was, a National Merit Scholar; surely there was not much more for me to learn, I arrogantly thought, even though I had the good sense not to say it.

"What do you mean?"

"I mean, when you become a Muslim and my wife, you will know how to handle all situations with dignity."

Wife? The word hung in the air along with the green forest car deodorizer and the Gloria Lynn coming from the speakers.

"Your wife? So we're getting married?"

"Of course. You didn't think I would make love to you without marrying you, did you? I'm a Muslim, and that would be fornication. I fully intend to marry you."

"And what about your wife?"

"Muslim law says I can have four wives as long as I can provide for them, but I'm not planning to have four wives or even two. I'm going to divorce Hafezza."

Shortly after we got back from Philadelphia, he asked his wife for a divorce and moved out of their house in East Orange and into a garden apartment on a tree-lined street a few miles away.

"You're doing what?" my mother screamed when I told her.

"I'm going to marry him when his divorce comes through. I only have two more months of school and I'm done."

"What about college? That Mount Holyoke been callin' every five minutes and I don't know what to tell them."

•

College was my mother's ultimate dream for me, and I knew the idea of my not going was a stake through her heart.

"I'm still going to college," I reassured her. "But I'm not going away. I'll go someplace close like Rutgers or something."

"Oh hell, girl, I can't believe you're throwing all your good grades away because of some ol' Moozlem. Girl, I don't know what is wrong with you. You ain't got the sense you was born wit."

"Mom, stop. I'll be fine. Don't you want me to be happy?"

She ignored me and continued her rant. "And who's gonna pay for you to go to Rutgers? You didn't apply for a scholarship from them."

"I'll figure it out, Mom, maybe he'll pay for it."

"Oh, he will, with what? After he gets finished payin' child support and alimony, he ain't gonna have much left."

"He can afford it." I tried to sound sure of myself with my mother, but I hadn't really thought all of this out.

"And I can get a work-study job, too."

I had never had a job before. My parents didn't want me to have even a part-time job after school because they were afraid my grades would suffer. I wasn't used to having to struggle. If I wanted something, a new leather jacket, boots, whatever, they got it for me. I got an embarrassingly large allowance for whatever minute chores I did around the house, like cleaning the dog's dish or raking leaves. I moved out right after graduation, he was in the stands, and my mother stopped speaking to me. My father acted as interpreter between my mother and me during the final weeks before I moved out. He said I was throwing my life away. My guidance counselor was apoplectic when I talked to her about passing on Mount Holyoke and Oberlin.

"Not many students here get that kind of opportunity, Alice," she had told me a few days before graduation while we figured out my final grade-point average. I knew she was right; most of the kids in my high school didn't even go to college. Most of them were going to jobs at the post office or to "work for the city" as government secretaries or clerks. All the kids who were merit scholars were going away somewhere, either to a southern Black school or somewhere in New England. Cheryl, who graduated second in our class, turned down Yale because she couldn't afford the room fees. She accepted the full scholarship from Seton Hall so she wouldn't have to worry about money and she could live at home and look after her grandmother, who'd raised her. Cheryl was barely speaking to me for changing my college plans.

"How can you take any man seriously who would leave his family? What makes you think he won't do the same thing to you?" she asked continually.

Cheryl was pathetically logical.

"You watch. We'll grow apart. You won't go to school, you'll get fat and boring, and I'll finish school and travel and make a lot of money, and I won't be able to be friends with you because we won't have anything in common," she had said.

Even though she didn't approve, Cheryl helped me move in with him the day after graduation. All I had was my two new Samsonite pieces that my mom had bought me for college and a few boxes of books, mostly paperbacks. I was scared about being there with my things and actually living with him. I'd never even shared a room before. I'd never cooked anything other than scrambled eggs, and I'd never even gone to the grocery store without my mother, but I was eager to learn all I had to to be a good Muslim wife, although I wasn't technically either. In order to be a member you had to receive an X from headquarters in Chicago. You had to send three letters there, copying exactly what they told you to say, and after six months to a year you were granted an X. If you had a common name like Linda or James, you would have a high number before your X because there were a lot of people with the same name who'd joined before you. The X represented the unknown last name that African Americans were stripped of when they were brought from Africa during slavery.

"So do you want something to eat?" I asked him after Cheryl had left us alone.

"No. I've got to go out soon."

"Tonight? But I just moved in. I thought we'd go out to dinner or order something in, to celebrate."

"We'll celebrate when I come back, Alliyah. I have some business to take care of at the restaurant. It won't take long."

I began to pout, and he came over and kissed my forehead, which was slightly covered by the chiffon scarf I'd begun to wear to cover my hair. I also wore wide pants and tunic tops designed to cover any curves in the body.

"I'll see you in a few hours," he said. *"As-salaam-a-lakium."*

I didn't say anything. I was pissed and he knew it and he left anyway. It was late June and the nights were getting hotter. There was no air-conditioning in the apartment, and the heat made me sleepy.

His key turning the cylinder woke me. I looked at my gold-plated Seiko that my parents had given me as a graduation present. It was midnight.

"Where were you?" I demanded.

"I was at the restaurant. There was a problem with a brother that we needed to take care of," he said, removing his suit jacket.

When he spoke like this, I knew not to ask for details.

"I apologize for not calling. Did you get yourself something to eat?" He put the jacket on a wooden hanger and hung it on the hall doorknob.

•

"No. I've been sleepin' since you left. I guess the move and everything made me tired. I wanna go to bed." I stretched my arms over my head and headed for the bedroom.

"Okay. I'll be right in."

No sooner had I put on a nightgown than the phone rang. The toner was up high.

"Yes," he said into the receiver. "*Walakum-salaam*. . . . Yes, she's here. . . . No, I'm not going to let you speak to her. . . . Please don't do that. . . . Listen, Hafezza, we've already talked about this. . . . Yes, I know it's difficult. . . . Okay. I will. Yes. I promise. . . . Sleep well."

He hung up the phone and I heard him sigh. I could tell that his wife had been crying.

The next day was Saturday, and Cheryl and I were going to Livingston Mall to get new clothes for her summer session at Seton Hall, part of the deal for scholarship students. He had left early that morning for FOI (Fruit of Islam) class. I was dressed and sitting on the sofa, waiting for Cheryl to pick me up. When the buzzer rang, I grabbed my bag and went to the door and opened it.

"Um, hi," I said to the stranger facing me.

"Salaam-a-lakium."

"*Walakum-salaam*. Do I know you?"

"No. But you know someone I know very well."

Oh, shit, I thought. She was nothing like I had imagined her to be. I pictured a small, demure woman, and here was this Watusi standing in my face. I didn't know whether I should slam the door and lock it or let her in.

"Would you like to come in?"

She pushed past me and looked around.

"So you're Hafezza? I'm Alice."

"I know damn well who you are, bitch, and you're sleeping with my husband, and I do not appreciate it, okay? So you can take your little self in there and pack up whatever you brought over here and go on back to wherever you came from," she said, hands on hips, neck motion in full effect.

"I think we should have a talk, Hafezza."

"I don't have anything to say to you other than you are living with my husband. He's my husband now and he's going to always be my husband. I don't know what he's told you, but we're not getting a divorce. We have children. We have a fam—" She broke into tears.

"We have a family," she said, and collapsed onto the couch.

"I can't let him go, do you understand that? Do you?" she yelled, wiping her tears with the backs of her hands.

I went into the bedroom to get some tissues. I felt like shit. I wanted him here to deal with his wife. I shouldn't have to deal with this mess. She took the tissues and wiped her face.

"I'll fix some tea. Do you want some tea?" I needed to do something with my hands.

I went into the kitchen to turn on the kettle, and she started talking to me from the living room.

"You know, I didn't plan on coming here. I called last night to talk to you, but he wouldn't put you on the phone."

"Yeah, I know. What did you want to say?" I walked back into the living room and sat down next to her.

"I know him. I know how slick he can be. I know how he has probably lied to you, and I wanted to just tell you my side of this."

"What's your side?"

"We've been married for ten years and every few years someone catches his eye and he has a little thing on the side. With the other ones I just turned my head because they didn't last long."

"You mean he's done this before?"

"Well, not moved out. He's never moved out of our home. I'm afraid that he might really be in love with you, but I can't let him go. I won't. He's the only man I've ever loved. He's the father of my children. We have a home."

The whistle summoned me, and I was grateful for the reprieve. I fixed two mugs of peppermint tea and carried them into the living room. I put the teacups down on a metal footlocker that was our coffee table. I was in shock. This was not the picture he'd painted of his wife or himself. He had told me I was the first woman he'd been with since he had gotten married and he'd told me his wife would just let him go.

"I'm so sorry, Hafezza. I don't know what to say."

"Just say you'll leave. It's time for him to come back home now."

The turning lock interrupted us. He walked into the apartment.

"Hafezza, what are you doing here?" His voice was lower than usual.

She started to cry again. "I had to talk to the sister. She needed to hear from me," she said, looking down at her cup.

"Hafezza, you shouldn't have come here. Come on, I'll take you home." He removed the key from the door and walked across the room to face her, ignoring me.

"I'm not going until you tell the sister that you can't live here with her anymore."

"Come on, Hafezza. I'm taking you home."

"No, no!" She snatched her arm from his grip, spilling tea on her pale peach skirt. "I'm not leavin' until you tell her. She's only a child. What are you thinkin' about, being with her? Tell her right now that you're comin' home."

"Now, Hafezza, you know better than to act like this. This is not the way a Muslim woman carries herself. Now stop this right now."

•

I felt as though I were watching a parent talking to an unruly child. I couldn't believe the way he was treating her.

"I'm leavin'." They didn't seem to hear. "I'm going shoppin' with Cheryl." I went outside and sat on the porch, waiting for Cheryl.

When I got home that night, he was sitting alone in the darkened living room. The only light in the apartment came from the street lamp.

"Are you all right?" I asked, throwing my leather purse on to the couch.

"Yes. I'm fine. How was shopping?"

"Okay. So what happened? Why are you sitting in the dark?"

"I needed some peace."

"So, what happened?"

"She calmed down and we talked and she left."

"So what's gonna happen now?"

"We're going to go on the way we are." He stood up and faced me. "Alliyah, this is a difficult process. You have to understand that. You also have to understand that I love you very much and I believe that you are my divine right mate."

"I want to believe you, but . . ."

He put his hands on my face and kissed my lips before I could finish talking. "You can't have any doubts about me or my love for you or this will never work. You must believe in me completely."

His power over me had been total. I inhaled his words and let him hold me tight.

Our situation ended one night in August when Hafezza came banging on our door at four in the morning.

"Open this damn door!" she yelled between bangs. "I'm not leaving until somebody opens this door."

I sat up in bed, not knowing what to do. I worried that our elderly neighbors would be scared into a heart attack. He got up and slowly pulled on a pair of suit pants—he only wore suits—and went to the door.

"Hafezza, why?"

She walked into the living room. She sounded overwrought. She begged him to come home and just cried and cried. I was watching from the bedroom and decided I was tired of this drama; it wasn't the first time she'd barged in on us. I wasn't willing to put up with his crazy wife, whom I didn't really think was crazy, just in love, a lot more than I was.

Suddenly I felt myself being released from his power and the pull of belonging to a movement. I had needed to feel like I was attached to something bigger and got caught up, like many did during the seventies, in the need to feel power, but I realized I didn't need a group. I had some force inside me to propel me on.

Monday morning I tracked down Mrs. Kauffman, my high school counselor, at her home in South Orange to find out if they would still have me at Holyoke. She made some calls, probably telling them that I'd been temporarily unhinged, and it worked. They reinstated my entrance and basic grant. I told him nothing. After two weeks of living together, it became very clear that he was not the man I wanted. Hafezza wasn't a liar, and what he did to her began to make me sick.

The next week I packed my stuff into my parents' Buick and we headed for South Hadley.

•

IF A PERSON IS able, during this long process, to experience that he was never "loved" as a child for what he was but for his achievements, success, and good qualities, and that he sacrificed his childhood for this "love," this will shake him very deeply but one day he will feel the desire to end this courtship. He will discover in himself a need to live according to his "true self" and no longer be forced to earn love, a love that at root, still leaves him empty-handed since it is given to the "false self," which he has begun to relinquish.

•

I was curled up on my Jennifer convertible sofa, reading this passage over and over from *The Drama of the Gifted Child.* I'd made a discovery about my childhood, our childhood, mine and Lucas's. We were our parents' cherished children for our achievements, not for who we were. Lucas probably knew this all along, and it explained why he was so crazy, rebellious. I just turned the anger inward, toward me.

It was a raw rainy Friday, and I'd called in sick. I needed time to myself to digest my life. Right now there was no place else I'd rather be, only I wished that my apartment were nicer. The carpet is old and cruddy. It's rust, and even after I vacuum it never looks clean, but the place is rent-controlled, and finding one of these in Manhattan is like hitting the lottery. It was mine.

Jack and I were moving along. Most of the time it felt good, and he seemed to find each new thing that I decided to share with him fascinating, instead of revolting, as I imagined. The Abdul thing, I'd even told him about my days at Holyoke when I lied about my father being a doctor, although I withheld his actual occupation. I knew Jack had never dated anyone like me, but as we got to know each other, it became clear that he'd had a lot of women. I was obsessed with Sherry, the one he'd almost married. I wondered what she looked like, dressed, how she walked. What her voice sounded like. I imagined her to be this perfect person, everything I ever wanted to be. How is this relationship ever going to work, I wondered, if he blew her off, in all her perfection? How can I, of no social standing or great hair, expect to hold on to him? What could he see in me that he didn't find in Sherry? I'm deluding myself. I should just end it with him, before he breaks my heart. What am I doing?

I got up to get some coffee ice cream out of the freezer, to eat it out of the carton. The phone rang.

•

"Hi, how ya doin'?" Jack's voice bounced through the line.

"I called you at work and they said you were sick."

"Yeah. I didn't feel like going in today."

"What's the matter?"

"Nothing. I'm fine. Just needed a mental health day."

"Oh. So what're you doin'?"

"Um, reading."

"Mmm. Uh, do you have plans for later?"

I didn't have a thing to do, but it was Friday night and I didn't want to seem like a loser. "Um, not really," I fudged.

"Good. Um, how'd you like to go to a party?"

"A party?" It was the last thing I felt like doing. It was raining, which meant my hair wouldn't hold up. I didn't feel like getting dressed up, but I didn't want to turn him down.

"Yeah, my mother is giving a little thing for my boy Jeff, I told you about him, he's moving here from L.A., and I have to go—"

I wondered why he was just getting around to inviting me. He must've known about this event before now. "So, what—"

"I had forgotten all about it, otherwise I would've asked you sooner. We don't have to stay long, but I need to see Jeff, and my mother would be furious if I didn't show."

"So what kind of party is it?"

"It's just cocktails. She wanted to throw something for him and invite all the department heads and docs from Harlem Hospital, where he's going to be on staff."

"It sounds fine," I lied.

"Great. So I'll pick you up about seven-thirty?"

"Fine. I'll be ready."

I hung up and looked around my studio. The bed seemed even more inviting than usual. Why did I say yes? I asked myself.

I usually started losing interest around the sixth month, but with

Jack, in month seven, I was still keen. I'd even glimpsed some of his faults—he was a little selfish, laid-back, and snobbish. I overlooked it. He was arrogant, but I decided that it was just confidence. He was not like Miles, and I wanted so badly for it to work out, so anything about him that might make me pause, I just ignored. Problem was, reading all this self-awareness stuff made it difficult to overlook me.

I was not looking forward to meeting Jack's mother. It was something I had hoped to avoid for as long as possible, but there was no way not to now. I knew this was going to be a test, and I wasn't sure there was a way to pass. From the way he described his mother, he was ambivalent about her, and if I liked her, he would probably see it as some fault in me, and if I didn't, well, she's still his mama and you can't say you don't like your man's mama. She sounded like a card-carrying member of the Black bourgeoisie, and I was sure that I wasn't what she'd hoped her precious only child would be with. The irony was, he wasn't really what my folks would want for me, either. My father would feel uncomfortable around him because he's a doctor, my mother would feel intimidated by all the family pedigree stuff. My parents would prefer my dating a college-educated guy who had a good, stable job, nothing too fancy, and someone who belonged to a church. Jack's mother would probably not approve of my looks; my skin is a little too dark for her and my hair a little too bushy. No guessing about my parents' race.

Jack showed up at seven-thirty and hated the suit I was wearing to his mother's. I was crushed because it was my favorite outfit. After he'd invited me, I'd hung up the phone and immediately begun agonizing over what to wear. I thought about my off-white wool suit, but that was too dressy. I'd considered a paisley long dress, but that was too hippie-dippie. A black cocktail dress was what Jack would want me to wear, but it was too predictable. I decided on my black pin-striped trouser suit. The jacket had a little Lycra in it to hug in the right places. I draped my new cashmere shawl over one shoulder, went bare underneath, added a string of pearls, and thought I looked fabulous.

Jack greeted me at my door with: "That thing looks like something Madonna would wear."

"So you don't like it?" Sarcasm drove Jack crazy.

"Why couldn't you wear a dress or a skirt or something?"

"You usually like the way I look."

"I do, but . . . I mean, it's nice, but for something else, not this. You're meeting my mother for the first time."

"I see. So you like the fact that I'm not a debutante, but you want your mother to think I am, at least the first time she meets me."

"Oh, forget it."

It was not a conversation Jack wanted to have. His mother, his feelings about his mother, were too convoluted. It was something I'd have to get him to talk about, I decided.

We rode in silence in the cab uptown. I looked out at his mother's block, and it looked like a movie set. The perfect limestones and brownstones had grand front entrances and gaslight fixtures. Pink and red geraniums hung from window boxes. There were brass nameplates with the date the house was built and ornately carved addresses.

"Oh, hello, son," Clair Russworm said, opening the heavy mahogany door. "How are you, dear?" She talked with her lips pursed and sideways so as to give her progeny the perfect air kiss. She was wearing an emerald green satin tunic over black satin slim pants,

•

large black plastic-and-fake gold bangles, and dangling gold earrings. She had on a pair of those fluffy feather high-heeled mules, which I'd never seen a person wear in real life. Her face was heavy with too light powder and bright red lipstick. Her hair was a mass of dyed red curls.

"I'm fine, Mother. How're you?" Jack held the door open for me to walk through.

"And you must be Alice." Clair was smiling. "It's so nice to finally meet you, dear. Jack speaks of you highly."

"Thank you. It's very nice to meet you, too."

I felt her eyes performing an X ray, examining my skin, my hair, my red fingernails. "Thank you for having me," I heard myself say. I was always overly polite when I was nervous.

I wished Jack had liked my suit, but I could tell from what she was wearing that I needn't have worried so much. She wasn't the cross between Lena Horne and Diahann Carroll that I'd imagined her to be. She looked more like a Black Norma Desmond with an addiction to Home Shopping Network jewelry. And she sounded more like Ethel Merman than she did Myrna Loy. What game was she playing with herself? I wondered.

"So Jack tells me you write for a newspaper," the inquisition began.

"Yes. I am a general assignment reporter for the *Beacon-Herald* in New Jersey."

"Ah, in Jersey, yes? Now, tell me again, Jack told me, but I've forgotten. Where are you from, dear?"

"I'm from New Jersey—Newark."

"Ah yes, I remember that now. Newark. Can't say I've spent a lot of time there. That must have been an experience. Growing up there?"

It was less than five minutes, and she'd managed to get in something that sounded like an insult. I felt blood flash in my face, but I had to stay calm.

"I guess, but I imagine growing up anywhere is an experience." *Bitch,* I wanted to add.

"Yes, perhaps. Anyway, dear, we'll talk more later. There's whatever you want to drink inside. Enjoy."

I'd been dismissed, and I'm sure I had failed her test. The least I could've done was seemed like a grateful darkie. Screw her, I thought, and went to search for Jack.

I walked into the parlor, where mostly older, elegantly dressed people were mingling. The mahogany walls were polished and framed pictures of Jack, in his various incarnations, were sprouting from the marble fireplace mantel. A tomato red satin love seat sat on an intense Oriental rug in the center of the room and was surrounded by real and fake American and French antiques. I stared at Jack's expressions in the different photographs. In each one there was the same half grin, four teeth barely showing. There's a slight sadness in his eyes that I'd never noticed in person. It made me love him. I scanned the room and located him.

"Hi, there you are," Jack said as I walked up to him and an attractive brother, badly dressed in a brown suit. "Meet my boy. This is Jeff. Jeffrey Doran, meet Alice Andrews."

"Alice . . ." Jeff pushed past Jack and took my hand between his. "It's a real pleasure to meet you. I've heard so much about you. Actually, the man can't stop talking about you. So what's your secret? My boy just does not carry on like this."

"Is that so? I don't know, Jeff, but I've heard a lot about you, too, endless tales about your exploits at Howard."

"Mostly about my brilliance, I'm sure?"

"No, mostly about the grain-alcohol parties you used to throw."

We all laughed.

•

"Uh-huh, well, dear Alice, that's just one of my many talents," Jeff said, stroking the lush black beard that framed his broad chocolate face.

Jeffrey Doran was from Brooklyn, the Fort Greene Houses, the projects. His mother had been a single mother who, on welfare, raised four children. Jeff had been singled out as the smart one and went to Brooklyn Friends Academy on an ABC scholarship. ABC—A Better Chance, he would later explain—was a group that tapped intellectually motivated kids from low- and middle-income backgrounds and sent them to top prep schools. Jeff and Jack met in undergrad at Harvard and went to Howard Medical School together. He was a lung specialist, who was about to marry Laura Green, whom he'd met in Los Angeles three months ago, where she was working as an assistant curator at the L.A. County Museum.

Laura entered the party like a breathless 1950s movie star. Patting her chest, she waved her chiffon scarf to us from the foyer as Clair Russworm took her raincoat and pointed her in our direction.

"Hi, sweetheart, I'm sorry I'm so late, but I had the most unpleasant cab ride," she said to Jeff while offering him her cheek.

"Oh, baby, was it really bad? Come here and let me give you a hug."

They did a small embrace.

"Now say hello to Jack and Alice." Jeffrey turned Laura toward us.

Kisses were faked, hands shaken.

"So, Laura, how's the museum business?" Jack said.

"Oh, you know. So much art, so little time."

Jack had met her once before.

Fortunately the crowd was thinning, and Jack felt that he'd

given his mom enough of a showing. After half an hour of sipping the same glass of white wine and listening to Laura go on about the most recent Chagall exhibit she'd seen, I was ready to leave.

"So you guys wanna go out to eat? Maybe Sylvia's?" Jeff said.

"Dinner would be great, darling, but can't we go someplace else? I can't stand all that greasy food," Laura said.

"I'm open. You wanna get some dinner?" Jack said to me.

"Sure," I heard myself lie. I'd rather have had Orville Redenbacher's for dinner.

"Okay, baby, where do you want to go?" Jeff asked Laura.

"How about Palio? Someone at the office was telling me about how fabulous it is."

I rolled my eyes and looked at Jack, but it was lost on him. He was game.

Palio is an expensive modern Italian restaurant tucked away in the Equitable Center. Cherrywood and a large modern mural surround minimalist tables and chairs.

"How about a bottle of wine," Jeffrey said, pushing in Laura's seat.

"Yeah, let's get the wine list." Jack motioned for a waiter.

"So, Alice, you're a reporter, I hear?" Laura asked.

"Yes, that's right."

The waiter came and Jeffrey asked him to recommend a wine, which he did, and it was ordered.

"Sweetheart, you should never ask the help to order wine for you," Laura scolded.

Jack jumped in and changed the subject. "Alice is covering this really interesting trial. This dentist is up for murdering his wife—"

"Really? Sounds gruesome," Laura said, sounding bored.

"Well, the gruesome part is how he killed her," I said.

"Yeah, he came home and found her performing fellatio on their six-month-old, snaps, and hits her in the head with a barbell," Jack said.

"Get outta here, damn," Jeff said while dipping his bread in olive oil.

"Can we change the subject?" Laura sighed.

She preferred to talk about her favorite subject, herself. She went on about how she missed Washington, her hometown, because there was something very comfortable about all the class stuff, even though she was from the wrong side of town—northeast—and didn't miss being dismissed by the Gold Coasters on the northwest side of town. She said it was easier to place people, even if all you knew about them was who their parents were. "You didn't have to bother to get to know them. It was also part of the tradition of D.C. It wasn't as if middle-class Black people didn't want to be Black, they just wanted to be seen as different from the negative stereotypes of the poor downtrodden so often shown by the majority media. Certainly, Alice, you, being part of the media, can understand that."

I took a sip of wine and smiled at her. She went on.

"There are just so many Blacks in D.C., it's just important to make distinctions since there aren't enough Whites or other kinds of people to make enough separate groups. It's just human nature," Laura said, and sipped her Barolo. "After all, there have always been house Negroes and field Negroes and there always will be."

No one touched what Laura said. It hung in the air like pollen before Jeff began stammering about an ABC benefit he wanted us to buy tickets for. He was on the board of ABC and had scholarships set up for several kids from his old housing project.

"Sure, man, how much is a table?" Jack asked.

"Five G's."

"Put me down for a table."

•

"Cool. My man," Jeff said, and reached to give Jack a high-five.

After Sambucas, we said good-bye to Jeff and Laura and hailed a cab on Sixth Avenue. In the cab Jack fumed about Laura. "Jeff wouldn't even look at a girl like her when we were in school," he said.

"Like what?" I asked, although I was still reeling from her house Negro–field Negro comment.

"Shallow. A serious gold-digger. She's the worst kind of striver. Those kinds of women were always hanging around the med school, trying to hook up with a doctor, and Jeff couldn't stand them," Jack said, loosening his tie in the cab.

"Mmmm."

"It's like he's completely whipped. I think all her talk, Bearden this, Vermeer that, turns him on. Like he thinks she's really cultured."

"Well, you never know what goes on between two people behind closed doors," I said, trying to sound objective.

"Yeah, right, and Jeff wouldn't know culture if it smacked him in the face. She's fucking him senseless, that's all it is, and then she's gonna bleed him dry after they're married, you watch."

I didn't know what to say, so I kept my mouth shut.

•

IT WAS A BRILLIANTLY sunny June day, complete with local saunalike humidity. The perfect D.C. day for Laura and Jeffrey's wedding. Clair Russworm's soprano carried "Ave Maria" throughout the cathedral, Blessed Sacrament, which looms over the D.C. border into Bethesda, Maryland. Clair had been an opera major at Howard when she had met Jack's father, who had been completing his medical studies. She had dropped out of school because they'd had to get married.

Laura looked appropriately radiant in a cap-sleeved, hoop-skirt wedding gown that was undoubtedly couture. The guys wore morning suits and top hats. The bridesmaids wore pink.

The reception was at the Regency, a newish hotel near downtown D.C. with a picturesque courtyard at its center. We were served champagne and hors d'oeuvres by gloved waiters as the bridal party posed for pictures in front of a man-made waterfall. Jack was the best man, so I was pretty much left on my own. I wandered around, smiling at strangers and eavesdropping. There was a cluster of Laura's overly powdered aunts who were providing commentary on everything from Laura's hairstyle, which was a simple bone-straight pageboy, to the flowers, white roses, to the bridesmaid's pumps, stilettos.

"Where did Laura say Jeffrey was from?" said Aunt One.

"He's from Brooklyn," said Aunt Two.

"Well, where in Brooklyn?" asked Aunt Three.

"I don't believe it was Stuyvesant Heights," Aunt Two said. "I think he's from, well, Brooklyn Brooklyn. He was a scholarship student."

"Well, it's just too bad that she couldn't have snagged that Scoffield boy, from that family. *He* would have been a catch," Aunt One said.

I wished that I had brought my tape recorder. Jack would never believe me if I told him what I heard. He was constantly trying to pretend that the class divisions were a thing of the past. I looked around the courtyard, and there seemed to be a thousand light-skinned men with light brown wavy hair and blue or green eyes escorting women who looked like their sisters, drinking Cook's as if it were water and debating about whether Martha's Vineyard was better than Highland Beach. The men looked like magazine ads for Polo and Britches in their kelly green, blue, and tan linen jackets, light socks, expensive shoes, and quiet ties. The women wore conservative chic jewel-toned outfits with coordinating shoes and purses in matching spring colors. I wore a funky olive-drab silk knit long skirt and matching short-fitted belted jacket, classic, clunky black Stephane Kelian pumps, and a satin backpack. One of the couples made their way over to me and introduced themselves.

"So, you must be from New York." I guess my wild hair, made more like Foxy Brown's 'fro thanks to the infamous humidity, and my offbeat-for-this-crowd outfit were clues.

"Yeah, I'm from New York. And you're from here?"

"Yes," they said simultaneously. "Three generations," he added, sounding satisfied, as if he'd just told me that he'd owned D.C. for three generations.

"Oh, that's nice," I said, not knowing how else to comment.

"I'm Chris Swift," he said, and extended his hand. "And this is my wife, Stephanie."

"I'm Alice Andrews."

"So you're with Jack?" she put in.

"Yes? You know Jack?"

"Yes, from the Vineyard. I think everybody knows Jack or who he is," she said.

"So, where do you live in New York?" Chris asked.

"Um, the Upper West Side. Do you know New York?"

"Very well. I went to Columbia Law school. Couldn't wait to get back to D.C."

"Yeah, well, you know, New York's not for everybody."

"And what do you do there?" he pressed.

"I'm a reporter."

"For?" he demanded to know.

"You must know Sharon Strong?" Stephanie piped in before I could answer.

"Uh, her name is familiar—"

"She's at *The Wall Street Journal,*" Stephanie said.

"Uh-huh, I've met her before."

"Um, I think she's like a copy editor or something. We went to Spelman together," Stephanie continued.

"Oh yes. We've met. We know a few people in common."

I wanted to get back to the everybody knowing Jack comment. I realized that Stephanie was probably a champion Negro Geography player and could be a great resource.

"So, Stephanie, you've known Jack awhile?"

"Oh, I've known him forever, you know, summers on the Vineyard, just hanging out."

"How do you know Jack?" Chris asked with that same prosecutor's tone.

"From New York—"

"Well, how'd you meet?" he wanted to know.

"We met on a plane."

"Really. Oh, that's nice. My cousin Tracy met her boyfriend on a plane and—"

I cut Stephanie off. I could see she was also a champion of the non sequitur. "You know, I see someone I need to say hello to. It was nice meeting you both."

I got away from them before Chris launched into a full interrogation and Stephanie proved her Negro Geography prowess. Folks from the tribe, D.C. being its capital, were amazing that way. They'd take the most tangential morsel and want to make a connection. "Oh, you shop at Safeway. Well, do you know so-and-so . . ." It was beyond tiresome. And the family tree questions were considered appropriate party chatter. Once at Holyoke, my freshman suite mate, who was from D.C., asked me a few days after meeting me, after she'd given up trying to guess my social class, what my grandfather had done for a living. I had to say I had no idea. She'd thought that was strange. No one my age had ever asked me what my father did, much less my grandfather. I would later realize that I'd entered into a new world, where that kind of question was pertinent. Initially when my suite mate told me about the Black middle class, I thought that I'd finally found my long-lost milieu. I had no idea then how far off that mark I was.

I wandered around the courtyard some more, hoping to meet someone who had read a book or even watched a nature special; judging by what I overheard, those things were not discussed. As far as I could tell, this group didn't even have a lively race discussion going, which was unusual for a gathering of more than three Black people, especially ones who didn't know each other very well. This place was a humid desert speaking not only meteorologically, but for ideas as well. Once again I was back on Fenton Avenue, not fitting in.

I found Jeff's mother, who was looking more out of place than I was feeling. Obviously no one had told her about the brutal D.C. heat. She was wearing a long-sleeved gold satin-and-lace waltz-length gown, white lace stockings with a pearl design on the ankle, and pearl-studded gloves. Beads of sweat formed a line above her lip.

"Mrs. Doran, are you having a good time?"

"Oh yes, baby. Everything's beautiful. I'm fine, just fine, 'cept my feet is about killin' me."

I looked down at the puffs of skin rising from dyed-to-match pumps. I felt for her and on some level imagined what she must've been feeling. Laura's family virtually ignored her, and there wasn't enough of Jeff's side there to make her feel comfortable.

"How you doin', baby?" she asked me. I walked her over to an empty wrought-iron-and-glass café table and had her sit with me.

The waiter brought us flutes of Cook's, which we both downed as though it were lemonade.

"So, what'd you think of the ceremony?" I asked. What I really wanted to ask was what she thought of her new daughter-in-law.

"Oh, it was just the most beautifulest thing I ever did see."

"Yes, it was."

She looked around, seeming like a junior high school girl at her first dance. I was personally invested in her feeling more comfortable; her level of belonging directly connected to my own.

"So you must be so proud of Jeff."

"Oh yeah. My Jeffrey. Always said he was gonna make me proud."

"That's nice."

"You got a nice fella there, that Jack."

"Yes, he is."

"Y'all gonna get married?"

"I don't know. We haven't been together that long."

"How long?"

"About eight months."

"Humph. Jeffrey ain't known Laura no mo' than three or four."

"Yeah, I know. I guess some people just know what they want."

"Yeah, and some people's just good at gettin' what they want."

Her comment took me by surprise. I'd slept Jeff's mother, underestimated her, but she didn't miss a thing. She was like the women in my old neighborhood who could size a person up in minutes, read them like the newspaper.

Jack was trying to make his way over to Jeff's mother and me but was being dragged around by his mother. When he broke free of her, he was still stopped continuously by revelers who seemed to want nothing more than to touch his hem. He was a celebrity in this crowd. Several older women in hats kissed his cheeks, patted his hair, and chatted him up. I hadn't been with Jack in a crowd like this before, so I'd never seen the Russworm thing in action. They treated him like Prince Russworm of the long-lost tribe of Freeborns.

"Whew, it's really hot, huh?" he said, plopping down on a wrought-iron chair after he'd finally made his way through the throngs. "Hope we're going inside soon. You having a good time?" he said.

"Oh yes, everything is just perfect."

"How about you, Mrs. Doran? Can I get you something?"

"Naw, I'm fine, baby."

"Are you done with the pictures?" I asked.

"Yeah, looks like it, at least for now. It's fun seeing all these old faces. That woman over there was a patient of my grandfather's, and her daughter is married to one of my dad's med school classmates. And my mother and that woman are club members—"

"That's nice. So they didn't need Jeff's mom to be in the pictures?" I whispered to Jack.

"Guess they're doing family pictures later."

"But I saw Laura's mom with you guys—"

"Mmm. I don't know." He brushed off my observation.

I wanted to have a good time for Jack. I felt like this was yet another test for me that I needed to pass, not for Jack, but for me. I needed to figure out how to do this without losing myself, but everyone seemed so focused on the exterior. How could a people, Black people, actually seriously adopt attitudes that our former masters had fed us for the sole purpose of dividing us and therefore keep us fighting with, disliking, and distrusting each other? It seemed insane to me that a people, twelve generations from one of the most inhumane systems of slavery in history, could actually be so cruel to one another. Maybe I was just too crazy for Jack. He probably needed somebody like that Stephanie woman, who seemed perfectly nice and had probably never had a bad mood or original thought in her entire life.

"There you are, dear, I wanted to introduce you to— Oh, Alice dear, forgive my manners. I didn't know you were here. How are you?"

"Oh, I'm fine, thank you, Mrs. Russworm, and you?"

"Wonderful. Mrs. Doran? Wasn't the ceremony lovely?"

"Yes, it was somethin'."

"So, Jack, Judge Carter is here and wants to say hello. Come with me."

Jack turned to me. "I'll be back."

We moved inside the hotel for a sit-down dinner, but before dinner would be served, we'd have to see the bride and groom have their first dance and the bride would have to dance with her father. I worried about Mrs. Doran dancing in uncomfortable shoes, but she did fine. It was Laura's mother I should've worried about. Laura's father, a pleasant enough, unimpressive sort, made his way through a clichéd toast about long life. Obviously not satisfied with his stamp on the couple, Laura's mother, the social engine of the family, who'd made more than a few trips to the bar, got up and stood before the microphone.

"I just wanna say to you all, dear friends and family, thank you for coming and blessing our Laura as she makes her new life with this charming man, Dr. Jeffrey Doran. I've waited all my life for this day. Ever since Laura was a little baby, I knew what I wanted for her. This is a fine young man, with an honorable profession. Take care of my baby." With that tears began flowing, and Laura and Jeff had to walk her mother to her seat.

I was seated at the table with other girlfriends, boyfriends, and spouses of the bridal party. The champagne was flowing, and so were the tongues.

"Well, I'm glad that's finally over," said Laura's sister's husband to another brother-in-law.

"The Queen of Sheba done got married."

"Man, be cool," said the brother-in-law, laughing.

Both men were wearing gray suits. The one doing the talking also had on a gray tie and gray shoes. He was married to Laura's older sister. Laura was the youngest child and, from what I could put together, had been groomed to marry a doctor. In many Black families, being a doctor, or marrying one, is what becoming a priest is in Italian families. It's as good as it gets. Nirvana. The men in gray both worked for the federal government. One was a GS-12 or -13. I figured, by the way they told me this, that it was something of an accomplishment, but they'd been treated like pigeon-do by Laura's mother because of what they weren't. I figured resentment had to be pretty deep for them to go on in front of me and the other strangers at the table.

"All I can say is, I'm glad they ain't gone be livin' here," the second man in gray said.

"Yeah, seems like our loss is Westchester County's gain. Look at her. She in hog heaven," the first man in gray said, referring to Laura's mother.

I wanted to pull out my pad and ask them questions about the family, but I resisted. Instead I went to the bar to get a club soda. The Cook's had given me a headache.

I went to the ladies' room to remove some of the oil that was now covering my face. Thankfully a bathroom attendant had a bottle of Drug Fair aspirin. I sat in front of a mirror after taking the pills to let them get to work. I looked at my hair, which was big and bushy. I looked not only as though I were from out of town, in this crowd,

I seemed to be from outer space. No one here would let their hair "go back" like this. I thought it looked kinda good, but two of the bridesmaids in pink who stood in front of the mirror next to me, with perms so straight they were afraid to revert, looked at me as though I had asked for spare change.

THE RECEPTION lasted into the night, with lots of dancing to a swing band. We flew back to New York the next day, with me nursing a hangover. Seeing Jack in his milieu had presented a picture of him that I'd tried not to see. I decided, after my Advil got to working, that we were going to have to deal with who we were if we were going to continue. At least he was going to have to deal with me.

"So, that was some wedding," I said after takeoff and some coffee.

Jack was wearing sunglasses and pushed into recline. "Yeah. It was fun. Did you have a good time?"

"Um, I had an interesting time."

He took off his sunglasses and looked at me. "How so?"

"Well, it was interesting seeing you in a different light. In that group."

"What group? What are you talking about?"

"I mean, the tribe, as you call it. Seeing how they all wanted a piece of you. You're like a celebrity to them."

"Aw, no. That's my mom's thing. I just know a lot of people."

"Jack, you know a lot of a certain class of people."

"Yeah, so?"

"So, I'm just saying it was interesting—"

"Yeah, but what are you getting at, Alice?"

"I'm not getting at anything. I just overheard things there that were kind of chilling and made me feel really out of place—"

"What are you talking about? You're just as much a part of that class as I am."

"No, I'm not."

"Oh, come on. You went to a good school, you have a good job, a profession—"

"Yeah, but I'm not a member of the tribe, like, you know, Daddy was a doctor, Grandfather was a doctor, that stuff—"

"Alice, how many times have you heard me go on about that stuff—"

"Yeah, I know you don't talk about it, you just take a lot for granted."

"Like what?"

"Like life is easy and fun and that everyone gets to do exactly what they want to do."

"Well, I realize that I have had certain privileges."

"Certain privileges."

"Okay, maybe many. So what. Do you want me to pretend to be something I'm not?"

"No. I just don't want you to be close-minded, that's all."

"You think I have a closed mind?"

"Well, it just seems that your world is a little small, that everybody you know has a similar background, one like yours."

"Jeff doesn't, and it doesn't matter to me."

"He's the only friend you have like that. All the rest of them are people you've known your whole life, who had houses on the beach, who went to Europe as teenagers, private schools, professional parents and grandparents. And they even all look a certain way. Take a look in your photo album. I'm the brownest woman you've ever dated."

"That's not true—"

"Well, those other darkies didn't make it into your book of memories . . . and you just make assumptions about people. You've made them about me—"

"Like, how?"

"Like about my background. You assume that I've had a certain middle-class upbringing."

"Well, that's right, what's wrong with that?"

"What's wrong is what you've made me out to be in your mind."

"And what's that, Alice?"

"That I'm some BAP or debutante or something."

"No, that's not what I think."

"So what do you think my background is?"

"Um, I don't know. Sort of middle, I guess."

"Jack, don't tell me you haven't thought about it."

"Well, Alice, I guess I have assumed a certain level—"

"Uh-huh, I know you have, and you're wrong."

•

"Wrong for assuming or for what I assumed?"

"Your assumption."

"Okay, so your parents are teachers—"

"No."

"So, what do they do?"

"My father is a mailman and my mother is a seamstress."

"So. That's not far from what I thought. Alice, despite what you saw in D.C., I really don't care about that stuff."

"I think you do and you just don't want to admit it."

"And why do you think that?"

"It wasn't just the way you were so comfortable in that group at the wedding, but in other things. I see how you cringe whenever I talk to service people, like Archie in your building, and that time we were stuck behind the garbage truck and the brother who was collecting garbage waved at me and I waved back, or how you didn't want to even deal with how Laura and her family were treating Jeff's mother at the wedding. And even your good school comment. I mean, I'm convinced that if I'd gone to a less prestigious school, you wouldn't even be going out with me."

"Oh, come on, Alice, where do you get this stuff?"

"Name one woman you dated seriously who didn't go to a top school and have a profession."

"I'm not going to answer that—"

"Can you? Can you name one?"

"Alice, this is silly."

"And what about that good hair comment you made that time about your grandmother?"

"What? What are you talking about?"

"You were describing how your grandmother didn't straighten her hair and you said she didn't even have good hair."

"Why do you remember this stuff? I mean, it's not about you."

"It is, Jack. I want you to see me, to understand where I come from, that my world is nothing like yours, but it's just as good."

"And you think that I don't think that?"

"Well, until a few minutes ago, you didn't even know about my background."

"Yeah, and now I know and it doesn't make any difference. I love you."

"You what?"

"I do. I'm crazy about you. I really don't care where someone comes from . . . Jeff is my very best friend and he's from the projects—"

"Who went to prep school and he's a doctor—"

"Oh, so I should go out and get some friends who aren't doctors and went to public school? What should they do, Alice, collect garbage? Know all about zip codes?"

His last comment stung.

"I'm just kidding. Look, Alice, the fact of the matter is people become friends based on common interests, bottom line. I guess in a different world I'd have friends from the working class, but frankly I have no interest in cultivating such. I like my life and my friends, you included, the way they are."

I felt myself beginning to sulk. I don't know why I thought he would admit to being an elitist.

We rode in silence for what felt like hours but was in fact only five or ten minutes. I didn't know what else to say, and Jack seemed to be chewing over things.

After the captain announced our descent, Jack reached over and squeezed my hand. "I really love you, Alice."

Just as I'd needed to tell Jack about my background, I also needed for him to say he accepted me. Now I was really confused.

• • •

•

When we got back to New York, instead of going home with him, I took a cab to my own place. I told him that I needed to read some clips to get ready for an interview the next day, which was true, but I didn't need an entire day to prepare. I needed to talk with Cheryl, my touchstone. He seemed disappointed but also kind of relieved, like maybe he needed to digest what had just happened between us, too.

I got home and my apartment was hot and funky. I opened a window, changed Essa's water, and dialed Cheryl.

"I'm so glad you're there."

"Hey, girl, what's up? How was the wedding?"

"Ugh, please, everything you thought and more."

"Details, please, only the gory ones."

"Well, the striving mother got drunk and made a speech, basically letting everybody know that her prayers that her daughter marry a doctor had been answered. . . ."

"No, she didn't."

"Yeah, she did."

"Eh, did you just wanna throw up?"

"No, actually I wanted more."

"You're really not well."

"I know. Then there were the programs."

"Uh-huh?"

"So next to the name of each member of the bridal party, they had their degree listed."

"No."

"Yes."

"You're lying."

"I wish."

"That is so unbelievably tacky. What else happened?"

"It was everything you'd expect from a colored wannabe society event. Spent easily fifty–sixty grand, even had a colored society reporter there. . . ."

"What, writing down the guest list?"

"Yeah."

"Well, was it fun?"

"No. It was painful."

"Why? You know not to let those silly people get to you."

"It wasn't that so much, it was seeing Jack in it. He's really a prince."

"Surprise, surprise. Where've you been?"

"It's one thing to know it, something else to see. He just takes so many things for granted."

"Yeah?"

"Like he thinks all poor people have to do is change their attitude and they can pull themselves up."

"Oh, now there's a sign of a horrible person."

"You know what I mean."

"Yeah, I know. He was born on third and thinks he hit a triple."

"Right. Things were just handed to him. Do you know he doesn't even have any student loans? His family was just able to pay."

"Well, Alice, if you really like the guy and he seems to really like you, so what, let go of all that other crap."

"I'm trying, but I don't know if—"

"I think you like feeling bad. You're looking for reasons to break it off."

"I am not."

"Well, what are you doing?"

"I just want to make sure everything's on the table this time, that's all. And I don't wanna get my hopes up and get disappointed again. I don't want to fall for him and find out he stands for everything I hate."

•

"Of course, that makes sense, but you'll just have to keep going to find out."

"He told me he loves me."

"What! Why didn't you tell me that first? Omigod. What'd you say?"

"Uh, nothing."

"Nothing? You didn't say it back?"

"No, I'm not sure. I don't know. Well, I'm pretty sure, but I don't know. I don't know if I can trust it. I know Jack has never gone out with anybody like me before. How do I know I'm not just some experiment?"

"You don't, and you won't know that he won't hurt you, but we never know that."

"Oh, you make me sick when you talk like this, you're so damn sensible."

"I know. I'm such a pain."

"I really think Jack is a snob."

"Yeah, he probably is, but does that mean he can't really love you?"

"But I'm not—"

"I know. It's our curse, we're not BAPs, Afrotiques, or commoners, but we deserve happiness, too."

We both laughed.

"So give the brother some slack, assume he is a snob, and go on seeing him. What's the worst that can happen? At least you know he has good manners."

"What a comfort."

"Hey, don't laugh. These things become important, 'cause when they don't know, they have a tendency to get mad at you for knowing."

"Oh, it's all so complicated."

•

"That's what makes it fun. Look, doll, I gotta go."

"Where you going? It's Sunday afternoon."

"I have a brunch date with a guy from my store."

"Oh, yeah? Cute?"

"No, but nice with good home training."

"Well, phew, wouldn't want you going out with somebody who doesn't know which bread plate is his. . . . Have a good time."

"Thanks."

I DON'T KNOW HOW I knew what I knew. Call it instinct or wisdom, but I had always known that I wouldn't stay in the world into which I was born. Maybe I just hated it so much, I'd unconsciously promised myself to find something else. At college I had envied people who couldn't wait to graduate so they could go back home and find a job, a spouse, a house, begin their life. What seemed so sure and appealing to them was, for me, a Sisyphean task. And the idea that I couldn't do it and didn't want to scared me, made me think there was something deeply wrong with me, that maybe I was some kind of new breed sociopath who had no consciousness of home. I knew that I wasn't unsentimental—quite the opposite, in fact.

To this day, I can still remember how sad I was when my favorite yellow sweater no longer fit. I had loved to wear this sweater, especially during the first weeks of school. It was hand-knitted cotton and had four covered buttons on it. It made me happy. But in the third grade, I had outgrown it, that was my mother's phrase. She wanted to give it away to some needy child, as she did everything in our house that we no longer used. Even though my arms looked like little fat sausages in the sleeves, I wanted to keep that sweater. I told my mother it would be a souvenir, like my souvenir Empire State Building pencil sharpener. But she thought my protests were nonsense and gave it away. Maybe that's where I learned to part with things that had become too small, like my life in Newark. Maybe the idea of wanting to hold on to things was too scary because I knew that I'd have to let them go someday. I don't know. I only know that when I finished school and came home to plan my life and met a guy whom everyone thought I should marry because my diaphragm failed, I remembered the yellow sweater, only this time the tight feeling was around my neck and I couldn't breathe. I couldn't describe it to anyone, other than Aunt Thelma, who always understood me and would say, "Baby, if that's what you want to do, then I'm wit cha." My mother had said I was crazy to pass on this man. "So what if he's got no sense of humor and he's a little stiff," she said. What she didn't say, but I was sure she thought, was, He's nice looking and a lawyer. Even Sidney, from my old neighborhood, who by this time was in drag every day, said, "Girl, it don't get no better than this." I never regretted not marrying him. I would've suffocated. I would've died.

When Cheryl asked me one day, a few years after I'd had the abortion, what I really wanted in a man, the only thing I could think of was someone who gets it, who understands me. Her own love life was the pits. The guy she had supported through AU law school who had dumped her was engaged to marry his secretary. Cheryl was stoic about most things, but after news that her ex was getting married, she was losing it. I had convinced her to come to New York, where I put her up in my bed, in front of the VCR. I rented every stupid and sappy movie I could find. We watched and consumed large amounts of Ben & Jerry's Heath Bar Crunch and Häagen-Dazs Cookies & Cream. After a week she was ready to go back home.

I wanted Jack to be that person, the one who understood, but after D.C. I began feeling less than certain. He hadn't traveled far enough from home, and unlike Miles, Jack couldn't do levels and seemed to have no desire to learn. I guess he didn't have to, but I began to question whether his world and his scope were too narrow. I was falling in love with him in spite of all of that. He was a rich kid, as I'd first predicted, but he seemed to get me—at least he tolerated my neurotic side, my mood swings. I had gotten past my initial fear of him, and we were now moving toward one year together, and I wasn't sick of him. That was a milestone.

On our way home in a cab after seeing Aretha Franklin at Carnegie Hall, we had that "What do you like about me?" conversation, which invariably leads to "What kind of relationship are we having?" which leads to stuff about the future. Usually I was the one who broached these talks. Most men viewed root canal more favorably.

"So, where do you see yourself in five years?" Jack asked as the cab entered the park at Fifty-ninth Street.

"Oh, I don't know, maybe living in London or Paris or in the country somewhere with a house and kids and a dog."

"And a husband?"

•

"Of course. I wouldn't have a baby without having a husband."

"Really? That doesn't seem old-fashioned to you?"

"Absolutely not. I had a father. I don't want to cheat my kid outta that."

Although my relationship with my father was not emotionally close, I believed in the importance of fathers to kids and hoped for a different emotional situation for my unborn.

"Mmm. Is that you or Mount Holyoke talking?"

"Well, I don't know how to separate those."

The cab pulled into the circular drive of Jack's building and the doorman opened my side. We were at the stage where if we went on a date, it was assumed that we would be sleeping at one or the other's apartment. In fact, we slept together five nights out of seven, and I had my own closet space for a few sets of clothes and two dresser drawers. I even had phone answering privileges.

"If a brother is lettin' you answer the phone, that is tantamount to giving you a ring, okay?" Cheryl had said.

Jack's apartment was a modern L-shaped one-bedroom with den, in Manhattan real estate parlance a two-bedroom. The foyer walls were lined with framed sepia-toned pictures of his ancestors, proudly posed, with Romanesque noses and vague Negroid features. The waxed parquet floor was covered with a large Aubusson, and an oversize cognac-colored leather sofa with matching love seat were the living room focal pieces. A rectangular glass-and-granite coffee table was covered with several pine boxes, *AMA* journals, and *Scientific American* magazines. The only nonmedical things he read were Clive Cussler novels and *The Wall Street Journal*. He had a lot of black lacquer—the torchère and the entertainment unit, with its major selection of country and classical CDs. An original Jacob Lawrence and several William H. Johnsons were on the walls, the latter inherited from Jack's grandfather, who had known the artist. His queen-size teakwood platform bed had a matching dresser and chest of drawers. The small white kitchenette with all state-of-the art appliances was never used, save for the coffee maker. Jack didn't expect me to cook, which was another thing I liked about him. Often I thought Jack was too good to be true. All the women's self-help with your love life books that I'd consumed over the years had me wondering—if he seems too good to be true, then he is. But just as often, I would think he wasn't good enough, that he didn't have enough edge or enough various interests. He had no interest in reading the credits after a movie. Medicine and adventure novels could get kind of boring.

"You hungry?" he yelled to me from the living room. I was in the bedroom, taking off my navy pants suit.

"I'm a little munchy."

"I'm starvin' like Marvin. I'm gonna order something. What do you feel like, Indian or Thai?"

"Thai."

"Okay. We'll get both."

"No, if you want Indian, I'll eat that, don't get two."

I came back into the living room, dressed in leggings and one of his T-shirts.

"I'm getting both. Now what Thai do you want? Spring rolls and what else?"

It was something that always pointed up our difference. Miles was extravagant to the point of foolishness—he had a Porsche with a car phone complete with call waiting and a fax, plus he carried a cellular. Jack wasn't ostentatious, but he was used to having whatever he wanted. Miles grew up poor, so he was just a kid in a candy store. All his accoutrements were toys to soothe a wound that would never heal. I understood it, but I'd never be able to fix it. With Jack, whatever he wanted he always got, things were nothing to him, and his sense of entitlement was sexy.

"So how about a little appetizer before the food gets here," Jack said as he began nibbling my collarbone. His babylike skin smelled like green and wood. I rubbed his head; his thick curls felt like Persian lamb. I pressed my braless chest against his, and he put his face in my cleavage and inhaled deeply while his hands were on my hips and our bodies were grinding together. His erection was bursting through his summer-weight wool pants. I reached down and undid his pants and pushed his Jockey briefs down to his thighs. He pulled my leggings down and dropped to his knees, putting his nose directly on my clit, rubbing it softly until it began to feel swollen and my legs weak. He pulled me down onto the rug and rubbed my breasts with one hand while he reached into one of the wooden boxes on the coffee table for a condom. He put it on and guided himself into me. The Aubusson was rough against my behind, but I quickly forgot about it. Jack's slow, hard movements made my clit grow fuller and fuller until I exploded. We both did.

The buzzer awakened us, and Jack pulled up his pants to open the door.

"Let's eat in bed," he said from the kitchenette as he put the food on plates and a tray and got a bottle of merlot from his collection. We ate on the bed, feeding each other and drinking wine out of one glass. After we ate Jack had a dreamy, contented look on his face.

"Alice, do you know how much I love you?"

I believed that he loved me, not because he told me, but because of the way he was with me, the way he held my hand when we crossed the street, the way he put his jacket around me when I got cold or held an umbrella over me in the rain. There was a preciousness in his way with me that I'd never had before, at least not to this degree and certainly not with Miles. Jack valued me, and I knew this. Sometimes the thought of it overwhelmed me, made me feel like I couldn't trust it or that there was something wrong with him.

"Yes, Jack," I said finally, "and I love you."

"So what are we doing? I mean, we spend all our free time together. I have shirts at your place, you have stuff here. I mean, I know what I want at this point in my life. I think we should do something solid."

Solid? I thought about that Ashford and Simpson song:

"Solid. Dum dum dum. Solid as a rock, dun dun dun dun dun, that's what this love is. . . ."

I guess they were after a zillion years of marriage . . . but Jack was talking about marriage or living together. I thought about Miles and how badly I had wanted to live with him, even though on principle I don't believe in living together. It's usually what men want to do when they can't make up their mind about you.

"What do you mean by solid?"

"I don't know, just that I wanna be with you. I think we get along, I just think maybe we should do something—"

"Like live together?"

"Yeah or something like that."

"Well, Jack, there's living together and there's marriage."

I knew I was pushing, and I wasn't even sure what I wanted, but I wanted him to be sure and I wanted him to want to do something formal.

"Well, would you like to do something like that?"

I was lying next to Jack with my head on his chest. I couldn't see his face, but I was sure his eyebrows were raised and his eyes practically shut. I felt his heart beating fast.

"Do something like what, Jack?"

•

He put his hands on my shoulders and brought my shoulders around so that we were facing each other. "Something like get married. I want to marry you."

It was weird. I felt happy, but not the way I had always dreamed I'd feel. I wanted to jump up and down, do cartwheels or something, but that wasn't what I felt. Instead, it just seemed all reasonable and calm, except for the flips in my stomach. I couldn't believe that this gorgeous, successful, smart guy from a very well-to-do family would want me. He could have anybody he wanted, but he was asking me. It was soon, I reasoned. Maybe this was just what he did. Didn't he leave Sherry practically standing at the altar? Maybe I should talk him out of this, tell him that we need more time, but I didn't want to say the wrong thing and blow it completely. This was like finding a great piece at a sample sale that you weren't sure you wanted to buy, but you knew it was a great find for the price and that if you put it down, someone else would swoop it up before it had left your hands. I had to say something, and I had to make it good.

"Jack, I love you and I think I should think about this, just a little. You know, it's a big step, and I had this yellow sweater. . . ."

"Of course we should talk about it, but what's to think about? What about a sweater?"

"Uh, I'll tell you about it some other time. It's just a test I give myself."

We hugged each other and I cried and tried to determine if I was feeling like a sausage.

ROBERTA AND FRED, my parents, had been passionately in love with each other. People used to envy them. I looked upon it with dread. I always felt like an intruder, like having kids was not what they wanted as much as it was some kind of acquisition, like owning a station wagon in the suburbs. Who knew how their feelings for each other affected Lucas, although the most obvious sign of damage was his lack of love for himself. He had always been an outstanding student, and while my parents provided him with an expensive education—the Pingry School and Bowdoin College—he resented them and paid them back by hanging out with the lowest types he could find. Girlfriends who had had several children by different men. Women with no ambition or education, guy friends who had problems with drugs and petty crimes. White guys he went to school with, many of them average, had a sense of entitlement, as Jack had. Lucas didn't. His proximity to them seemed to make his life worse rather than better, as my parents had thought. My mother either couldn't see it or didn't want to. She pretty much dismissed us once we were able to take care of ourselves. In my case that was high school; for Lucas, he seemed to still crave Mom.

I pretty much stopped going home after my sophomore year in college. I'd go home with a roommate or a boyfriend for holidays. In the summers I'd waitress in Boston, just to avoid having to spend a summer at home with my mother, who, after the Abdul thing, had cut me off. But now that I was thinking about getting married, I was filled with feelings of family and I wanted her approval. I wanted her to see what I'd done. Whom I'd managed to get to fall in love with me enough to want to marry me.

I called to invite her to lunch.

"What should I wear?" was my mother's first question.

"What kind of place is it?" was her second.

After I provided her with what were crucial details, I hung up, feeling sorry that I'd made the date. To her, appearance was crucial.

Cafe des Sports is an old-time, straightforward French restaurant in downtown Newark. I knew its rustic charm would be lost on my mother, who now went in for more nouvelle Gothic interiors, like gold lamé place mats with matching napkin rings. She arrived wearing a red suit, red stockings, red pumps, and a floral silk blouse.

"Girl, you sure do know how to pick these outta-the-way

places," she said, putting her pocketbook on the floor and looking around.

"The food's good," I said, trying unsuccessfully to not sound defensive.

"Better be. They need a coat of paint."

"So, how are you, Mom?" I tried to change the subject and sound mature.

"Oh, fine. Everything's just fine. How you like my suit?"

My mother made all of her clothes, and while she was an excellent seamstress, her taste had become less conservative with age and now ran more toward the flashy, flame-retardant variety.

"It's nice."

"Thank you."

"How's Dad?"

"He's fine. Gotta lose some of that weight he's put on since retirin'."

"Uh-huh."

"So, what you got to tell? I know you didn't just invite me to lunch to talk about your father."

"No. I, um, have some news—"

"Oh God, what's wrong?"

"No, it's not bad news."

"So?"

"I'm getting married."

"Married! You? This I gotta see."

Her words felt like a Mike Tyson left.

She threw back her head as she patted the ice water that had dribbled outside her mouth. "So who is he? Are you gonna bring this one around for us to see or do we just meet him at the church?"

I was surprised by her bitterness. I didn't know she cared

enough to try to make me feel bad for not coming around. I didn't really think she'd noticed.

"Well, Mom, of course you'll meet him. His name is Jack—"

"What's he do?"

"He's a doctor—"

"A doctor. Well, ain't that somethin'."

It was worse than I'd imagined it would be. I was sitting with the woman who gave me life and all I wanted to do was run screaming from the restaurant, jump into my car, and drive to Manhattan and never again return to this dingy city where I was born.

Instead I simply withdrew from telling her anything more. We ordered lunch and ate in silence. After the meal she patted her mouth and thanked me. She told me my father would be picking her up across the street, in front of Bamberger's. We touched cheeks to say good-bye.

I'd been estranged from them, and too much time had passed. We couldn't have lunch and have it be the way it was with friends. We were strangers, and I blamed her for it. She'd pushed me to do well in high school and pushed me to go to Holyoke. She'd wanted to create this person she had wanted to be and, in the process, ruined any mother-daughter bond that should have been there. I was scared but could never tell her because to her I had everything going for me. It was a gulf that I had no faith in ever bridging. I wished I could chalk it up to generational differences, but that had never been a problem for me and my aunt Thelma, my mother's sister, who was more my mother than my mother. She would be happy for me. She would say the right things.

"Alice. Alice. Shouldn't you be up?"

I rolled over on my back. Jack was sitting on the edge of the bed, fastening the alligator band of his Cartier tank to his wrist.

•

"I'm so tired. I don't know what's wrong with me."

Jack looked down at me and pushed at my glands and felt my forehead.

I'd just moved into Jack's apartment after accepting his proposal, but I kept my apartment because I wasn't ready yet to give it up. Jack thought it was stupid to continue paying rent, but it was what I needed to do for now. Things had been going along fine, until I started wanting to have a warm family life and reached out to my mother. After that lunch with her, everything began annoying me. Even the way Jack touched my forehead. It reminded me of being in elementary school and how my mother questioned me when I said I was too sick to go to school. She believed you never missed school unless you were bleeding from your eye sockets.

"Does anything hurt?" he asked.

"No, nothing hurts. I just don't feel good, I don't wanna go to work."

"Well, maybe you should just stay in today. You want me to call the paper?"

"No. I can do it."

"Okay." He leaned in and kissed my forehead. "I'll see you later."

He rose from my bedside, grabbed his blue blazer and the *Journal* from the floral grandma chair I'd moved from my studio apartment.

"Bye," I called after him, trying not to sound as pathetic as I felt.

I rolled over to Jack's side of the bed and picked up the phone and called the newsroom. Betty answered the phone, *"Beacon-Herald,"* with food in her mouth.

"Betty, hi, it's Alice, can I speak to Larry or Steve?"

"Sure, hon, hold on."

"Larry Stein."

"Hey, Larry, it's Alice. I'm not feeling too well. I'm not coming in today."

"Oh, all right, Alice, is everything okay?"

"I'm just feeling a little fluey. I'll check in tomorrow, all right?"

"Cool. Feel better."

I hung up and wrapped myself in covers. I hated my job, hated my boss and everything that was making me think too much. I realized how ill prepared I was for life with bumps. My mother had raised me to believe if only I went to school, made it through college, knew how to present myself, the world would be kind, life would be easy. Sure, I didn't have her life, with horrible racism and extreme poverty, but I still had to deal with shades of the same monkey. Racism was still a factor. Larry Stein treated me and the other Black reporters like ambassadors to the dark ghettos throughout the state, not as trained professionals. He'd more than once questioned my ability to be objective. Once when I was covering a graft trial of a Black councilman I found out that Stein had grilled another reporter who had been in the courtroom one day about the things I'd written. I was fatigued from constantly having to justify my actions to White co-workers who were clueless about Black people. Who thought we came in one of two varieties: Huxtable Black or welfare Black.

"Oh, so you're like *Cosby Show* Black, right?" More than one actually said that to me. And then there were my own, Blacks I did end up covering who live in bad situations and leered at me as if I were the cause of their misfortune. Often, I felt like monkey in the middle, a game we used to play on Fenton Avenue, where you stand between two people who play catch over your head and you have to get the ball. On days like this, I felt like the ball and contentment were equally elusive.

•

THE PAGE-ONE above-the-fold *Beacon-Herald* Sunday feature infuriated me. It was about how top colleges were scrambling for Black students who had scored high on their SATs. The implication was that smart Black students were as rare as bald eagles. There was only one line in the story about the test possibly being culturally biased and not one mention of the large majority of White students who take prep courses, beginning practically when they're in the second grade. I fumed over the paper; it was my paper. My colleagues wrote this stuff, and I knew a lot of them felt this. Usually, I kept this kind of feeling away from my weekends, but my rage was spilling over into the rest of my life. I looked over at Jack, sitting peacefully, sipping orange juice and reading the sports section. I closed my eyes, trying to calm down, and began thinking about my own SAT experience. I'd scored high enough the second time, but I hadn't even known that there was such a thing as a *Princeton Review* or any other prep course. I wondered how many Black kids had. Clearly, that was why more Whites were doing better; they were more prepared, period. The phone shocked me out of my muse. Jack didn't make a move for the phone; he never did, said it was part of his medical training to tune things out.

"Hello."

"Alice?"

"Yeah. Who's this?"

"It's Mom. Mommy."

"Mom. I didn't recognize your voice. Do you have a cold or something?"

"No, no. I'm all right. What are you doing? You busy?"

"We're reading the paper. I had just drifted off, Jack's immersed in the sports section."

"Well, I have some bad news."

"What happened? Tell me."

"Lucas . . ." She started crying. I knew something horrible had happened because my mother never cried. My mouth got dry.

"What, Mom? What happened?" Jack turned from the newspaper and looked at me.

"Lucas was in a car accident and he's in serious condition. We just came back from the hospital. They won't let us see him yet. He's going to have another operation and he's losing blood and . . ." She started to cry harder. I was stunned. I didn't know what to say.

"What hospital is he in?"

Jack took the phone from me. "Hello, Mrs. Andrews, it's Jack. Listen. Do you remember the doctor's name who's working on Lucas? . . . Okay. I'll call there and see what I can find out and I'll call you right back. . . . Okay. . . . Okay, bye."

I had locked my arms around my legs and was rocking on the leather couch. Tears were rolling down my face, but I didn't brush them away. My brother was always fucking up, but it was never anything serious, he always managed to escape without a scrape. Even with all of his wrong jobs and running up credit cards, he always managed to land on his feet. He seemed omnipotent in a way.

Jack massaged one of my shoulders and softly patted my cheek. "It'll be all right. I'm going to call the hospital."

He dialed the cordless phone and walked into the den. I couldn't make out all of what he said.

". . . in the belly? . . . What time? . . . Uh-huh."

It occurred to me that I'd never seen Jack in his work context and how amazingly different he seemed. Since we'd become serious, after our first month or two together, he'd left all of the social decisions, from what movie to see to which friends, up to me. Now I was watching him take complete control. I knew that he was strong and confident, but I'd never seen this particular brand of sureness. Jack stood in the doorway between the den and our living room, holding the phone in one hand and running his other hand through his hair. For a moment everything about him was turning me on. For a second I forgot about Lucas. I wanted to fuck Jack. I scolded myself for being an insensitive bitch and again adopted something resembling concern for my brother.

"What?" I said when Jack hung up.

"It doesn't look good," he said, sitting down next to me on the sofa. "Lucas has lost a lot of blood and suffered a major head and belly trauma. The car went down a cliff—"

•

"A cliff?"

"Yeah. Somewhere around Paterson. They're about to lap him . . . I mean, take him back into the OR for a second procedure."

"Did you talk to his doctor? I mean, what are they doing? Did they give him a transfusion? Does he need blood? What kind of blood does he have?" Suddenly I was filled with concern for my brother, the one I used to be so close to a long time ago.

"I think we should go to the hospital."

"Is he going to die?"

"They don't know yet, Alice. I'm going to call your mother back."

I gathered my things, Coach sack, my heavy wool cardigan from college, and threw in a cotton turtleneck and gray Holyoke sweatpants. Jack and I walked fast down the hall to the elevator. We rode to the garage, holding hands but not talking. In the car, I looked out of the window as we traveled uptown, through the park at Ninety-seventh Street. It was early fall, but the leaves were already oscillating. Jack drove down the bumpy West Side Highway. I thought about Lucas and how, when we were little, we used to roll down the hills in Weequahic Park. It was my favorite thing to do. I would start to wheeze and Lucas would try to stop me, but I wouldn't. I loved feeling the freedom that rolling down hills gave me. It was like free-falling.

When I was born Lucas was twenty months old. He was smart and very aggressive. My parents had told me that they'd showered him with presents when they brought me home because they were afraid that he'd be jealous of the new baby. In fact, the opposite happened. They said he loved me and called me his baby. We became like twins; I remembered we had the same O positive blood.

They'd always made sure he did well in school, won at science fairs and spelling bees. They thought it was important to develop his mind because he was a boy. Me, it was enough, they said, that I was pretty. But I figured out, early on, that pretty was not something my family valued all that much. Everyone was good-looking, so it was sort of taken for granted; besides, beauty had been something of a curse for Grandma Viola, my mother's mother. Grandma Viola had been a beauty—tall, broad shouldered, with what the old folks call good hair—and it had just caused her grief. Grandpa didn't like the idea that other men looked at her prancin', his word, through their tiny South Carolina town. On the days when she got too much attention, he'd beat her. One day the White man Grandma worked for, doing daywork, told Grandpa that if he didn't stop hittin' on Viola, he'd run Grandpa outta town. Grandpa was not one to be threatened, even by a White man in the 1930s. That night when she came home from work, he beat Grandma till her whole face was just about all blue and blackened. About a week later the White man showed up at Grandma and Grandpa's shed and took Grandpa for a ride. The next time anybody saw him again, he was dead.

Jack pulled into the circular driveway at University Hospital, in the heart of Newark. A guard came over to us, and Jack flashed some kind of medical ID. We found Lucas's floor and saw my parents sitting in a small, cramped waiting area.

"You got here so fast," my mother said.

"How's he doing?" I said to them.

"The doctor just left, that's him," my father said, pointing toward a squat man walking down a corridor, away from where we stood.

Jack asked my father for the doctor's name and then headed off after him. We were left with each other, the hum from the soda machine providing the only sound.

•

Jack returned after twenty minutes with the update. Lucas had lost a lot of blood and had already received a transfusion. It would be a good idea to donate more, he said.

"I'll give some. We have the same kind," I said.

"Good. Let's go find out where they take it."

We left my parents in the waiting area. I was relieved to have something to do.

Within a week, Lucas recovered from the surgeries but was still in serious condition. Tubes and a respirator were hooked up to him. His face looked peaceful, and his skin was so clear that it seemed translucent. My mother was a wreck. My father was even worse. Jack was amazed that he'd survived this long. A good sign, I thought. I was pretty much in shock, both by the accident and by my parents' reaction. Lucas got away with murder, but I'd always chalked it up to my parents' indifference. The way they basically moved into the hospital showed me a different side. Just when it seemed Lucas was getting better, he contracted pneumonia. It was Sunday, a week after the accident. My parents and I were in his room, reading the paper, staring. His breathing became labored, and the nurses cleared us out of the room. A red alert was sounded and a doctor came running down the hallway, his lab coat flying like Superman's cape. The nurses, three West Indians, cleared us out of the room.

"It's probably just a machine malfunction," one nurse said, trying to reassure us. "Don't worry. He's been doin' real good," she continued.

I looked at my watch. They'd been with him for ten minutes. My father was holding his head in one hand. My mother was leaning against the wall, looking up and praying with her eyes closed. I gripped my sweater, which I'd rolled into a ball and held against my chest.

•

I looked at my watch again. Five more minutes had passed. I knew the longer they worked on him, the worse it would be. I felt as though this were happening to someone else and I was just watching, like one of the West Indian nurses. I locked my eyes on the large Seiko wall clock, watching the red second hand work around the face. Three minutes, then four. Five. Twenty minutes they'd been in there. I wanted to call Jack, but I was frozen. My father was crying now. My mother was bowing and praying. I walked over to her and patted her back. I couldn't think of anything to say. I looked at the clock; the hand moved mercilessly. Five more minutes. The doctors worked on Lucas for twenty-seven minutes but couldn't resuscitate him.

The child is supposed to bury the parent. When it happens in the reverse, it's an imbalance, like a hailstorm in July. My parents had to be sedated at Lucas's wake and the funeral. I seemed as if I were putting on a strong front, when in fact I didn't feel like falling apart. I felt sad, but not overwhelmingly so.

Jack held my elbow as we walked up the aisle of our small Solid Rock Baptist Church. A large woman on the organ played solemn-sounding funeral music. I was relieved that my family met Jack under circumstances that distracted them. I couldn't handle dealing with my mother's inappropriate questions or my father's sulking. There were stands of various arrangements, mostly of carnations and gladioli. Jack's mother sent pink roses and lily of the valley.

Lucas had been having problems for a while now. They should've known something was wrong when he ran up the credit card they gave him to use at college just for emergencies. When he bought a sailboat, they fussed a little but I think secretly liked the idea that he wanted one and was just so brazen about getting it.

"You know what Lucas has gone and done now, don't you?" I

had overheard my mother saying in a conspiratorial tone to Aunt Thelma over the phone.

"Lucas knows how to sail, even bought a boat while he was up there in Maine," my father would say to the man who owned the corner newspaper store.

Family lore was that Lucas would have been a success if he had been born White; then his telling the CEO of General Foods where to get off would've been seen as heart or spirit. Coming from a Black man, it was seen as uppity. Lucas had lived his whole life in denial.

Lucas's death forced me to start thinking about my own life and all of the compromises I'd made in my sorry career. I wasn't pushing myself and told myself that they were racist and there was no point. And they were racist, but there was a point, and it was my fulfillment, my happiness. If I wasn't going to find fulfillment at the paper, then I'd go someplace else. That was the future. Lucas's death also made me think about my past. I would have to deal with it before I could really move on.

After Lucas's funeral, life seemed to move in slow motion. I felt tired all the time, but my mother and I seemed to be moving toward one another. I had volunteered to help her go through Lucas's things and stopped by one day after work. We were in his small three-room apartment, once the attic of my parents' house before they'd renovated it for him when he moved out of his girlfriend Denise's apartment. They didn't break up, he'd explained, but he'd had to leave because her three children, none of them his, each of them by a different man, were just too wild. Lucas was a neat freak, and there wasn't much to go through, only a box of things that had never been unpacked and a small, light blue stationery box on top of his chest of drawers. I opened the box, assuming it was stationery that I would take. Inside there were five envelopes, each with a neatly handwritten name scrawled across the middle. There was one for my mother, my father, Aunt Thelma, his girlfriend, Denise, and me.

"Oh God, Mom, look at this. There're notes in here from Lucas."

My mother took her time, slowly folding the chenille bedspread that she'd taken off the bed, and walked over to where I was standing, holding the box. "What is that?"

"Look. I think you should sit down."

My mother sat down and looked at me. I opened the one addressed to me and began reading it to myself.

"What is it?" my mother asked in a tone that said she really didn't want to know.

"Um, it's a letter, uh, let me—"

"Gone and read it. I gotta do somethin' downstairs."

"Okay. I'll finish up here, then come down."

I sat down with the letter, not taking my eyes off the paper, and started again, from the beginning.

Dear Alice,

I'm sorry you have to find out like this that I decided to take my own life. It was something I've thought about off and on for years. Ever since freshman year in college. I've hated my life for so long. Everything I've tried didn't work out. The corporate route, the entrepreneur stuff, my relationships with women. I never could find a place where I felt I could be myself and be accepted. Not with Blacks, not with Whites. I always felt like I had to choose, at school where all the Blacks hung together, the Jews, the Wasps, the Italians, the gays. There was no place for me, for me to just be accepted. It was like life wanted me to be different than who I turned out to be. I was just supposed to be a good corporate sol dier, get a job and work it like Dad for forty years. But I couldn't do that. If I didn't kill myself, I would have probably killed someone else. The rage I've felt, that's been building up for the last twenty years, just exploded. This seemed like the best thing I could do. I didn't want to hurt anymore. I didn't want to hurt anybody else. I know what I did to you when we were little was an awful thing and that I hurt you. I want you to understand that I never meant to hurt you. I loved you more than anybody, including myself. You were everything to me. Your smile, your laugh, the way you used to stick up for Sidney when me and my friends used to call him a fag. You were just the best. After I did that thing to you, I really began to hate myself. I don't know why I did it. I wish I could say it was adolescent horniness, but I don't think so. Those girls at school were more than willing to let me do whatever I wanted to them. I guess I just wanted to be closer to you. I don't know. Anyway, I've made a mess of my life and figured Mom and Dad would finally be better off being rid of me. When I think about Dad working all that overtime at the Post Office just to send me to school and how I acted—running up their credit cards, trying to fit in, pretending I was something I wasn't—it makes me sick. I just hope you find peace in this life. I know I'll see you again. And I want you to know I will always love you and I'm forever sorry for what I did.

Always,

Lucas

I sat in the fraying taupe armchair and looked down at the light blue stationery. I marveled at Lucas's neat, tiny scrawl. Other than the campus shrink, I hadn't told anyone about what Lucas did. At the time I didn't even know what sex was. But I figured it was something bad because of the way he acted. Come here. Close the door. Don't tell anybody. I think we were called for dinner and I sat at the table with my head on my elbow. It was the first time my mother didn't yell at me to take my arm off the table. I knew how much I wanted them to love me, so I swallowed it, the way you swallowed a jawbreaker that hadn't melted enough and hurt when it went down.

I would have to tell my mother that her son had committed suicide and also that he'd tried to have sex with me when I was ten. I didn't think I could break all these things to her at once, but I also didn't think I could keep it in anymore. Lucas had freed me.

I went downstairs and found my mother in her ironing room. The smell of steam and spray starch was so familiar.

"Mom. I think you should probably read Lucas's letter."

"I don't think I want to right now." She didn't look up from the pillowcase. "Why don't you tell me what he said," she said.

I paused, going over in my mind a way to tell her. "Lucas didn't lose control of his car. He drove off the cliff on purpose. It was a suicide."

She sighed, too weak to do anything else and didn't say anything for what seemed like forever. "Did he say why?" she finally uttered.

"No Mom, not in mine. Maybe in the letter to you he explained more. Do you want me to read it?"

"No. Your fatha can read them. I don't wanna know."

"There's something else, Mom."

"What else could there be?" She stopped pressing and set the iron upright.

Once I told my mother my horrible secret and she received it with silence, I had to get out of that house. It was the usual cold sixty-five degrees, yet I was burning up. I felt as if the wind had been knocked out of me. I lied and said I had to cover a zoning

•

board meeting and left. I drove home, taking the turnpike, into the Lincoln Tunnel, across town on Thirty-sixth Street, up Park, and into our garage, all the while wiping my tears and snot on my linen shirtsleeve. I felt angry and ashamed, but I also felt relieved.

I was grateful for the empty apartment when I got home. I drew a bath, poured a glass of stale merlot, and sobbed some more while I got into the near scalding water. I just wanted to step outside of myself for a while. I wanted to be able to put my brain on a pillow and give it a rest. I heard the door slam. I cursed my decision to leave my apartment.

"Hi. You home?" Jack yelled, and threw his keys on the foyer table.

"I'm in the bathroom." Why did he have to scream?

"Are you okay?" he said, sticking the top of his head in the opening of the ajar bathroom door.

"Yeah. I'm okay."

"Doesn't sound convincing."

"Really, I'm fine." I cupped my hands in the water and let it run over my face.

"You wanna go out to dinner?"

"No."

"Why?"

"I don't feel like it."

"You just said you were fine."

"Well, I'm not, okay?"

"Is it Lucas?"

"Yeah, and other stuff."

"Anything I can help with?"

"No."

"You wanna try me?"

"No."

"Why not, Alice?"

"Please close the door."

"Goddammit, Alice. I hate when you get like this. What the hell do you want? I'm here, I'm trying to be supportive. I don't know what else to do."

My bathwater had gotten tepid, as had my desire for a bath. I got out and wrapped my white terry-cloth robe around me and pushed past Jack. I flung myself onto the bed and pulled the comforter over me.

"Jack, I know I'm supposed to be happy and grateful to have you and this beautiful apartment and a job in my chosen profession, but I'm not. I'm miserable and I just want to stop feeling this way. Something is wrong and I've gotta fix it. As much as you hate it when I'm like this, I hate it even more."

"Well, you seem to like wallowing in whatever it is."

I hated when he talked like this. He didn't have a clue about what I was feeling, but he stood there all smug and superior. I wanted to slap him.

"You know, I've been thinking that maybe I should move back to my place until I figure this all out."

"Alice, if we're going to be together, then whatever the problem is it's my problem, too. Are you saying that you don't want to be with me?"

"I'm not saying that. I don't know what I want, but it doesn't seem like a good time to be making big life changes."

I heard these words coming out, and it was as if they were coming from someone else. I wasn't really prepared to break up with Jack. I didn't even think my problem had anything to do with the relationship. It was just me and my feelings that I needed to deal with. The conversation had taken on its own life, and I had no control.

"So you don't want to marry me?"

"I love you, but I don't think we should do anything permanent right now. I'm not in any shape," I heard myself say.

"Well, I know the Lucas thing has been traumatic."

"Jack, my brother killed himself, and yes, it's difficult and traumatic, and I'm also dealing with some other stuff."

"Killed himself?"

"Yeah. It wasn't an accident. He did it on purpose."

"Aw, man. I'm so sorry, Alice."

"Then there's other shit."

"Like what? Tell me."

"Incest."

"Incest? What incest? What are you talking about?"

"Lucas forced me to have sex when I was ten. It's been buried, I never thought about it or talked about it until now. I found his suicide letter today—"

Jack came over to the bed and put his arms around me. "I'm so sorry, baby. I'm so sorry this happened to you—"

I began to cry into his chest.

"I want to help you, just tell me what you need," he said.

"I don't know."

"Do you want to talk to someone, maybe a therapist?"

I agreed. I probably would've agreed to anything at that moment. I felt so relieved just to have told someone, other than my mother, what had happened. The walls didn't shake, and he didn't jump up and run away from me. I was moved more than I'd ever been. He made the appointment for me to see a therapist the next day.

•

THE PSYCHOLOGIST'S office was on University Place in the Village, and she looked like Alice Walker, with a rectitudinous face that was wise. I saw her one week and agreed to see her for the next six to see if we got on.

"Do you have any thoughts about what we talked about last week?" she asked during my second visit.

"You mean about the incest?"

"Well, that's not quite what I was talking about, but let's explore that. What have you thought about the incest?"

"I haven't thought about much else."

•

"And what are your thoughts?"

"I guess I just wanna know how it's affected my life, you know, like how does it play itself out in my relationships, my reactions?"

"Go on."

"Well, I guess that's why I'm here, 'cause I wanna figure it out."

"How do you think it has affected your relationships?"

"I don't know. I'm angry a lot, I don't feel really close to anybody, except maybe Cheryl and sometimes Jack."

"Yes, well, the anger is a classic symptom of an incest survivor. Is there anything else?"

"I read that one of the traits of an incest victim is shame. Is that true?"

"Is that how you feel? Ashamed?"

"Well, I didn't think I did, but when I look back at some of the things I did in college, like lie about my background and some of my responses now, to Jack and his background, there's probably some of it there. I imagine if it weren't for the incest thing, I wouldn't feel so much anxiety, like with Jack's mother, I'm sure I'd view her in a completely different way. And I probably wouldn't feel threatened by Jack's old girlfriend, who comes from a family like his."

"So his ex-girlfriend and his mother make you feel how?"

"I guess like I have to prove something, like I feel I have to prove that I'm good enough for him."

"And how do you do that?"

"I'm always trying to look perfect, be perfect, say the right thing. I'm too self-conscious, and then being that way makes me angry because I can't just relax."

"What do you think would happen if you just relaxed?"

"I don't know what that feels like. It's like when I had to be on guard all the time in school, when I was growing up, I had to pretend to be tough in order to fit in, so the rough girls would like me, and then in high school I became the princess that the kids in elementary school said I was, and in college, well, I've already told you about the lying in college."

"Well, you're on the right track by thinking about these things. I know it's painful, but it's necessary. Our time is up today, but I want you to do something. You should write down all you can remember of times you overreacted to things. And I'll see you next week. Okay?"

"Fine. I'll see you next week."

I had taken some back time off from work. It was due me, so I didn't feel guilty. After my session I decided to walk home. It was a moist fall day, the kind that brings hordes with boxed lunches into the park. On my way up Sixth Avenue I stopped at Bryant Park. The city had cleaned it up, planted daffodils, put in new antique-looking black benches, and granted permits to vendors selling upscale drinks and sandwiches. Lunchtime was over, so I had my pick of spots. I plopped down on a bench facing the back of the library. I took off my tortoise-shell sunglasses to rub my face. As I was putting my glasses back, a familiar frame entered my view.

"Hey, stranger," he drawled.

"Miles. Hi. What are you doing here?"

"Well, that's a helluva greetin'."

"Well, you're the last person I'd expect to run into in the park, in the middle of the day, especially on this side of town."

"I know, I never come over here, but I needed a walk, just finished my second all-nighter and the deal still ain't closed."

Miles was a master of the universe, an investment banker specializing in mergers and acquisitions. I hadn't seen him in about a year, since I'd started seeing Jack.

"So whatcha doin' out here? Daydreamin' again?" He sat down next to me.

"Nope. Just taking a break in my walk home."

"So you've moved, I hear."

"Mmm-hmmm."

"On the East Side now. Never thought I'd see the day you left the Upper West Side."

"Yeah, well, time for a change."

"He must be some man."

"I guess he is. So who told you?" I knew there were a number of people who could've told Miles about my new address and about Jack. Our world was tiny.

"Can't remember who it was. You know New York, it's just a small plantation for us darkies who can read and write."

"Yeah," I said with a sigh, choosing to overlook Miles's sarcasm, focusing instead on the truth of it. It was often used as hyperbole, that Blacks of the upper class all knew each other or of each other. Within the clique, investment bankers were like star athletes, and, as in the NBA or NFL, there were groupies. Miles was a top draft pick, as a VP fast on the way to managing director status. Women chased guys with incomes like his, just as the Laker Girls went after the pros. Of course, there were women investment bankers as well, and they were also forced to compete for the attention of brothers of their own ilk. It created a vicious, incestuous little world.

"I hear you gonna marry this guy," Miles said.

"Yeah, that's the plan."

"I don't see that rock," he said, playfully picking up my hand and holding out my ring finger.

"We haven't gotten around to that yet," I said, trying to sound casual but wishing I had a big rock to flash.

"What did I hear, he's a doctor or somethin'?"

"I know you know exactly what he does, Miles."

He let out a sinister laugh. "Yeah, baby, you know they got to give me the dude's résumé. So what kind of medicine?"

"He's a general surgeon."

"Mmmm. A surgeon, so he's a cowboy, huh. And where does he practice?"

"Mount Sinai."

"Very nice. And where'd he go to school?"

"Miles, why don't you ask me if he's a nice guy or if he makes me happy—"

"Whoa, baby, calm down—"

"I am calm, I'm just so sick of you business-card-flashing, Armani-suit-wearing, portable-phone-having assholes that I wanna scream."

He patted my hand. "Now, now, baby, obviously you're under a lotta strain. You still workin' out?"

"I'm fine, I'm just, oh, forget it—"

"Look, you wanna go get a drink somewhere? What's 'round here? The Royalton?"

"No."

"Well, you know, we could drop down to that little place in Saint John you like."

"Miles, really—"

"Okay, okay. Can't blame a brother for tryin'."

"I appreciate the offer, but no thanks."

Walking home up Madison, I was, as always, struck by how clean the streets were compared to the rest of Manhattan. Miles and the sun had given me a headache. How could I have spent two years with him and actually thought I was in love? Of course, the sex was crazy—in Riverside Park at dusk, at the Paris movie theater, in the elevator in his apartment building. I'd never wanted anybody the way I wanted him, but that never failed to be the case.

•

The more inappropriate someone was, the better the sex. After all that sweating and panting, I couldn't talk to him. Couldn't share the million and one thoughts I had a day or my equally numerous feelings. He certainly wouldn't be able to handle what I was going through now. He was a meat-and-potatoes kind of guy. No weird foreign foods or feelings for him, but he still made my thighs weak.

He was right about one thing: I loved the Upper West Side. I missed it. I would've traded it more happily for the Village, but the East Side—I hated it. I never felt like it was home, I always felt like people were staring at me, either White matrons who were checking out my clothes and trying to figure out how a nanny could afford to dress this way or real nannies who were trying to figure out who I was to be living in this neighborhood. Jack liked the West Side, too, but complained about the crowds and the homeless people.

"The East Side is just so much more civilized," he would say.

It was one of the things that made me question being with him.

ONE THING I LOVE about living in New York is that it's a walking town, and nothing clears things up for me like putting one foot in front of the other and setting out. You can work things out or just watch people, the other thing I love about the city. The people. You could walk down the street with a shaved head and an eye painted on your forehead and draw virtually no attention. I worked out all of my major dramas by walking. Feeling strong, maybe that's what it is. After a good fifty-block walk, I feel as though whatever it is, I can do it. I decided to stop doing diet pills, walking. I used to take them to stay awake right after college, during that lapse with the "marrying well" set. I finally decided to break up with Miles after many walks. Now, I could see the brush clearing. Lucas's dying had freed me in a way. I needed to focus on me and make sure I was doing right by me, before getting deeper with anything else, including Jack.

I got home and decided to go visit my aunt Thelma. Like walking, she always provided clarity for me. It was something I suddenly had to do. When Jack got home from the hospital, he found me packing my Coach duffel.

"So how long are you going for?"

"I don't know."

"And where are you going?"

"I need to see my aunt Thelma. I need someone I can talk to."

"What about the therapist? Isn't she helping?"

"I think so, but this is different. It's not intellectual. I need to be around someone who knows me, Jack, I mean, really knows me."

"And what about me?"

"Jack, this isn't about you."

"I mean, can't you talk to me?"

"Yeah, but, well, it's different. She's the mother I wished I'd had."

"So you don't know when you're coming back?"

"I'll call you from there. My aunt's number is in the book in the kitchen."

"And I'm supposed to just wait by the phone until you call?"

I leaned over the bed and zipped up the duffel. Jack was sitting in the floral grandma chair, looking at me as if he couldn't process what was happening.

"Look, I'll call you when I get there. And don't forget about Essa. Just feed her once a day, okay?"

•

Essa was looming, looking suspicious. I was sure she wasn't looking forward to being alone with Jack.

"Essa, give Mommy a kiss." She got away so fast that her legs were a blur of fur X's.

"Are you going to kiss me good-bye, Jack?"

"You just expect me to sit and wait until you decide to give me some attention? Do you realize it's been almost a month since we had sex?"

"Jack, I've got to get me together, okay?"

"That's all you think about is you. What about me?"

"What about you?"

I was sorry I said it as soon as it came out. I could feel the sting from my words. He said nothing and made no movements. He just stared. I felt a deep anxiety in the pit of my stomach. I realized that he saw my need to talk to my aunt as deserting him, and while it wasn't that, I didn't have the energy to explain. I resented his neediness right then.

I pulled on my denim jacket and hoisted my bag off the bed. Jack didn't move to help me. He didn't even look at me. "I'll call you later," I said.

Once I was out the door and at the garage waiting for Archie to bring the car around, I realized that while I was gone, Jack would also have time to think. He could change his mind about me and very easily pick up with any number of beautiful, intelligent, less complex women, and I would be but a mere memory. But I couldn't stay.

Tears welled up and I bit my bottom lip to keep Archie from seeing it tremble. He careened the car in front of me and smiled. The cross chiseled in Archie's gold tooth made me smile every time I saw it, which was often 'cause he grinned a lot. I jumped into my Saab and ground into first.

•

• • •

Cape May is the southernmost town of the Jersey shore, a three-hour drive and a lifetime from Manhattan. Aunt Thelma's white colonial, where I'd spent most summer weeks of my youth, stood as a raft to my drowning soul. In this overdecorated house, where the walls were covered with bad oil paintings and macramé by local artists, I could always find clarity. She was my mother's older sister and my favorite aunt. I don't remember how she won that distinction because she wasn't what anyone would ever mistake for a sweet aunt who baked pies and favorite cookies. She hardly cooked at all. She ate fruit and raw vegetables mostly, a habit formed when she was a live-in for a White family in Bedminster. She couldn't stand to eat her own cooking, especially food she was paid to fix. She was now retired after working for the same family for thirty-five years, ever since she'd finished high school. After twenty years, she had been promoted to be the nanny for the children of the woman Aunt Thelma had helped raise. She still had dinner with the family once a month and talked to the woman on the phone a couple of times a week. Aunt Thelma never had children of her own, but she had had three husbands, all working-class dreamers who couldn't keep up with her. She always said she couldn't find a man who was smart enough. She didn't go beyond high school, but she was one of the smartest people I knew, and she was industrious, too. She always had some new way to make money. She owned three houses: the one she lived in; a large green Victorian with pink shutters in the center of Cape May's tourist center, which, with help from her gay stepson, she'd turned into a profitable bed-and-breakfast; and an apartment building in the family hometown, Elizabeth.

She always had a wad for me. When I graduated from high

school she showed up after the ceremony and handed me a man's black nylon sock with $500 rolled up in it. "And don't do nothin' stupid," she said. When I finished college, it was a thousand. "I don't care what you do with it, just don't do nothin' stupid." She was the reason I didn't have to have a job in college, sending me money so that I could dress like a BAP. She was equally generous with her advice. "Girl, don't you ever marry no man who don't love you more than you love him. You courtin' disaster if you do."

She was the first real eccentric I ever knew. When I was little and we'd spend weeks together, she would let me stay up late, eat pizza three times a day. She even let me wear fingernail polish. She'd let me have sherry and we'd sit up in her huge brass bed, stacked with three mattresses, and play blackjack. When I got older she taught me to play bid whist.

She always wore big round dark sunglasses, like Jackie Onassis circa 1970, and a scarf around her hair turban style, exposing her widow's peak. The only makeup she wore was dark red lipstick. Her chestnut brown skin was flawless. I loved her so much because she always made me feel important.

The car making a U-turn in the gravel let her know I had arrived. She was standing behind the back screen door when I got out of the car. She looked the same: red lips, flawless skin, sunglasses.

"Lock your doors," she said in her rasp. "We been havin' robberies down here. Those damn college kids and their stupid frat parties be bringin' all kinda trash down here." There were never any mushy displays between us, but she was always standing there, behind the screen door, as soon as she heard the gravel crunch. We always kissed on the lips, which was a tradition in our family, but that was all the affection we ever exchanged.

"I got some grapefruit here. One of my neighbors brought them up from Florida. Or you could have some oatmeal," she said as I followed her through the narrow hall to the front of the house.

"No thanks. I'm not hungry. So how you doin? What were you doing?" I said, settling down on my favorite chair on the sun porch.

"I was sittin' in the kitchen, doin' the crossword puzzle," she said, pulling some pillows from behind her back on the wicker love seat. "So how's my girlfriend doin', and what you doin' all the way down here?"

"I was just out driving. I needed to get out of New York for a while."

"Uh-huh. Where's that Jack? You two fightin'?"

"No."

"You want some ice cream? I want some ice cream. Let's go in the kitchen."

The kitchen was for soul talks. We got up, and I followed my aunt's scruffed steps to the kitchen.

"So how's that job? You get promoted yet?"

"It's all right," I said, tasting the butter pecan. "I'm thinking about quitting," I blurted out as if I were seven years old and had to tell her that I'd broken one of her beloved fake Tiffany lamps.

"Oh yeah, and why is that?" She took in a tablespoonful.

" 'Cause I just don't wanna do it anymore."

"Well," she said, her mouth full of ice cream, "I hope you can come up with a better reason than that, 'cause ain't no reason for somebody like you to be quitting a job like that. You doin' what you went to school for, which is a lot more than most of these fools running round here can say. They treat you okay and the money's all right, right?"

"Well, the money's just okay. It's hard to explain."

"You mean, it's hard to explain to me. You don't think ya ol' auntie can understand what it's like to have a professional job like the one you have."

"No, Aunt Thelma, it's not that."

"Well, since when you can't explain somethin'?"

She had put me on the spot, and she knew it. I did think she was too unsophisticated to understand my problems with work and with Jack, but I really needed to talk with her about everything, including Lucas.

"I don't know what I'm doing, and sometimes I feel like I'm going to have a breakdown. I'm cryin' all the time, and when I'm not, I just feel like beating the shit outta somebody. I feel rage for no apparent reason, then I feel bad because I feel like I should be happy because I have so much."

The crickets and locusts were making their nocturnal calls, and the sounds reminded me that I could rest. Aunt Thelma pushed away from the kitchen table and walked over to the window. She patted the dirt in her potted peonies that were perched on the windowsill. I had the same broad shoulders she had. We had the same body shape, except she was only five three. For sixty-six, she was in great shape. Her shoulder blades poked out of her black knit sweater, which she had pulled over her beige linen capris.

"First of all," she said with her back to me and sounding like God, "you are not havin' a breakdown. We don't break down. We may make other people do that, but we don't, so you cannot have one. That woman I worked for, she has breakdowns, which is why she calls me every damn day, 'cause she can't figure out nothin' for herself and she's been given everything her whole life. You, my little girlfriend, come from folks so damn strong-willed that they had to leave the South or White folks was just gon' be forced to kill 'em. You couldn't have no will like that and be a Black man in the South, you understand that. Now, I don't know all of what's bothering you, I do know you can figure out how to get what you want from that paper, and if they can't give it to you, then you go look for somethin' else, and when you find it, then you leave, but you don't just git up and go without someplace else to go. Now, about Jack, y'all got to understand you both Black, plain and simple. You come from two different kinds of families, one had a pot and the other one didn't, but both of 'em is Black, and as long as you live and breathe you gonna be treated that way, so you two need to stop whatever foolishness goin' on."

I sat at the kitchen table, tracing the daisy design on the plastic place mat before me. I didn't know what to say, but I knew she was right. How she knew what some of my issues were with Jack was part of why I needed to see her. She always just knew. I wanted to tell her about Lucas, but I was afraid that she'd just say get over it. She turned around to face me.

"So, do you wanna go for pizza?"

It was her way of lightening up on me.

"Nah, I'm kinda tired from the drive. I'm gonna call Jack and let him know I got here okay and then I'm gonna go to bed. Maybe we can go for pizza tomorrow, okay?"

"That's fine."

I gave her a hug, even though it was not part of the family code. "Night, Auntie."

"Night, baby."

At the top of the stairs, I walked into the guest bedroom that I always used. Everything was the same: the white chenille bedspread, with the red, white, and blue crocheted throw folded neatly at the base, the nubby, olive green love seat, and the white vanity with mirrored tray covered with bottles of Jean Naté, Wind Song, and her beloved Joy. The little pink tufted stool was underneath. I went into Aunt Thelma's room, picked up the red Princess phone that sat on her nightstand.

"Dr. Russworm," Jack answered my page.

"Alice Andrews."

"Hey, how are you? Did you get there all right?"

"Yeah, I'm fine. You busy?"

"No, not now, I just finished up in OR. I'm actually about to walk out. I'm meeting Jeff for a drink."

"Oh yeah. How is ol' Jeff?"

"Aw, I don't think he's doing so hot. Laura's really givin' him the blues."

"What a shock."

"Yeah, I know. We all saw it coming, well, except Jeff. So how's your aunt?"

"Oh, her usual firebrand self."

"So, when are you coming home?"

"I don't know."

"Alice, running away is not going to solve anything."

"Jack, please don't lecture me. I told you I needed to get away and see my aunt."

"Fine. I'll see you when you get back."

He hung up. I held the red Princess receiver to my cheek and tears bounced off my face and onto my hand. I hung up and turned to see my aunt standing in the doorway.

"I'm fine, really," I said, trying unsuccessfully to wipe my tears before she could see them.

"I can see that," she said sarcastically. "What'd he say?"

"He doesn't understand what I'm going through. He tries, but he can't."

"Men don't have the equipment, but if he loves you, he'll try."

•

"Auntie, when I was ten—oh, you know, this is stupid. I'm gonna go to bed."

I touched her shoulder, said good night again, and went into the guest room. I took off my long rayon dress and my socks and sneakers and got under the covers. The pressed white cotton sheets were as good as those at the Four Seasons and probably as old as me. The smell of air-dried laundry made me feel safe to close my eyes.

AFTER A FEW DAYS with my aunt, walking arm in arm along the boardwalk, going to an Audrey Hepburn festival—*Breakfast at Tiffany's* and *Charade*—and playing cards in bed, my head felt cleared and my mood was better than it had been in months. I told Aunt Thelma about Lucas, and she said she understood how horrible it must have been. "Those things happened all the time to girl children in the old country"—her term for the South—"but you gotta let it go to save yourself. You don't wanna end up like Lucas. You're a survivor. He wasn't."

•

Her career advice was succinct: "I know these crackers still got they hangups, but believe me, girlfriend, things is a million times better than they used to be. Now you can take that to the bank."

I headed home. It was true. I was a survivor. In many ways Lucas and I had had the same issues of not fitting in, pretending. But now I was a grown-up. The girls waiting to beat me up were all gone. I could be whatever I chose, and I didn't have to answer to anybody. I didn't have to fit into a category, I could make my own.

I slipped in a tape of Anita Baker's *Rapture* and sang all the way home. By the time I was halfway there, my voice was sore from straining and I felt happy.

The next morning, wrapped in Jack's flannel robe, I stood barefoot on our cold tile floor and wiggled my toes. Our tiny modern kitchen was so flooded with morning sun that sometimes I put on sunglasses. I thought about my aunt and Audrey Hepburn and their sunglasses. Jack's welcome home last night had worn me out. He had early rounds at the hospital, as I slept in. I ground some beans for coffee, opened the front door to get the *Times,* and pulled up a stool at the kitchen counter. Leafing through the paper, I waited for the coffee to brew. The flannel caressed my bare body.

I had a second interview set up today with a magazine called *View*. On a whim, a few weeks before I had taken the time off from the *Beacon-Herald*, I'd sent them my résumé. They had called me immediately, and I had had an interview one day on my way to work. They'd seemed quite hot for me, and while I knew this wasn't my dream job, I needed to leave the *Beacon-Herald*. The work was no longer fulfilling and didn't pay enough. I had a $15,000 Visa bill—accumulated while buying Miles expensive presents and clothes for myself that I couldn't afford. *View* would mean a $10,000 increase plus a thousand-a-month expense account. Also, I figured my anxiety level would be much lower at this job, since I would be doing mostly fashion and my most taxing writing challenge would be coming up with lots of synonyms for "hot."

I poured mocha coffee into my favorite blue-and-white ceramic mug, stirred in the half-and-half, and waited a few seconds for the coffee to cool. I lingered over the paper, sipping my coffee, savoring my mood. I actually felt happy. I was glad to be back home with Jack.

I stood before my closet, deciding what to wear on my interview. My black Armani jacket with the charcoal wool skirt always worked. It had cost me two months' rent. I had been seriously depressed when I bought it.

Holly Thomasson looked as though she were born to be a New York magazine editor. A natural brunette who had successfully converted herself into a blonde. I would never understand White folks' obsession with blond hair. Mention that a woman is blond, and that immediately translates into beautiful and desired. The paler the hair, the better, it seemed, I guess the idea was that it was the farthest from dark. She was also superthin, another ruling-class obsession. Thin was the only standard of beauty for women's magazine editors and their subjects. Her uniform was a starched white cotton shirt with a little black skirt and square-toed, chunky heeled loafers. She wore tiny gold hoop earrings and no signet ring this time, but she did have the requisite large round diamond abutted by equally hefty dark blue sapphires on her left ring finger.

"Alice, hi, it's so nice to see you again, come on in. Do you want some coffee?"

Holly emphasized every syllable of every word, as if she were speaking to someone who didn't understand English. Unconsciously I started speaking that way back to her.

"Yes, it's nice to see you, too. I'd love some coffee," I heard myself say even though I was still shaking from overdoing the morning's dose. I should've asked for tea or decaf, but I didn't. Good corporate soldiers drank coffee and did not upset the corporate culture. I followed her into her corner office, which was decorated tastefully in shades of mauve. We sat on the sofa, and she crossed her legs and leaned in to me.

"So, your résumé is very impressive. You went to Holyoke? I went to Simmons."

We were about to play White Girl Poker. Worse than Negro Geography was White Girl Poker. Holyoke is more celebrated than Simmons, so she had to raise me, asking personal questions, referring to my résumé for more info to best me.

"So you live on the East Side? So do I." To make sure it wasn't Yorkville, she asked, "You're on Eighty-fifth between . . . ?"

When I told her Madison and Park, she ended the game. Not revealing her address meant I'd won the round. If I'd been wearing a wedding ring, she would have moved on to husband roulette, as in "What does your husband do?" But she, by dint of birth, won the set.

An overdressed Black woman reeking of Obsession and carrying a silver-plated tray with two china cups and saucers filled with coffee, a creamer, and a sugar dish came into my view. She was Holly's secretary. She gingerly placed it in front of us on the Lucite coffee table and left. I tried unsuccessfully to make eye contact with her.

"Thanks, Gloria," Holly yelled after her. "So, what do you think of our little setup?" she said, handing me a cup and saucer.

I was in my best interview mode: up but not perky, cool but not aloof. "The offices are great, and people seem happy," I said.

"So do you think you'd be interested in working at *View?*"

What I wanted to know was would I have an office with a window.

At least she was direct. I liked that. It could be fun, I told myself, maybe I could even get Gloria, Holly's secretary, to look me in the eye.

"Yes, I think it would be a challenge to come here," I heard myself say. I'd say just about anything now to get away from the paper.

"Well, great. We'd love to have you as soon as you can come aboard. Your references looked good, but we will need a few more, maybe five in addition to the ten you already gave us. Is that okay?"

Fifteen references. If I were a White girl, even one who had gotten her degree through a matchbook correspondence course, five references would've been sufficient. I knew, and she knew I knew, that this reference thing was saved just for us—Black people. Even though I don't fit the stereotype of a gun-toting, drug-selling ghetto dweller, I was still Black and had to prove that I could fit in. It wasn't about doing the job. The issue was, what kind of Negro was I? Was I agreeable or angry? I knew I had to grin and bear it, because it was just part of the Black tax, part of why Lucas checked out.

"Sure, five more, that's not a problem," I said.

"Well, great. I still need for one other editor to meet you, but I'm sure she'll think you're just terrif, too."

Terrif? What was I getting myself into? I looked around the office and wondered if it was too late to ask for an additional ten thousand. Holly called the other editor to tell her we were coming by. After a brief meeting with the production editor, a humorless woman in Birkenstocks, Holly walked me to the reception area. She shook my hand enthusiastically and said she was looking forward to working with me.

When I got to the elevator Gloria was standing there. This time she looked me in the eye and said hi.

"Hi, I'm Alice."

•

The elevator opened before us, she got in first, and we were alone.

"So, Gloria, have you worked here long?"

"Mmm, yeah, almost ten years."

"Ten years, really? So, I guess you like it here?"

"It's all right. These girls is a trip, but they okay. You gonna be workin' here?"

"Um, it looks like it. Unless one of my five additional references says that I'm really an ax murderer."

The elevator had delivered us to the lobby, but Gloria seemed to want to continue the conversation. "How many references they ask you for?"

"Well, first ten, and today they asked for five more. Why?"

"Man, that's the kinda shit I'm talkin' about. They don't do that for them White girls, three references is all they ever ask them for."

"Really? Are you sure?"

"Hell, yeah. Who you think has to Xerox all that shit, résumés and whatnot? I know where everybody went to school, they grades, reference letters, everything—"

I felt sick, like I wanted to throw up, but it was tempered with gratitude that I felt for what Gloria had confirmed, what I'd always believed but couldn't prove. Another standard, a higher hoop to jump through, if you're Black. In that split second, though, I knew I was still going to take the job, so I had to be careful not to let any editor come by and see me talking with Gloria as if we were old homies.

"Listen, Gloria, I appreciate the information. I'll take you to lunch—"

"You still gone take the job?"

"Oh, yeah, I'm taking the job."

"You go, that's right, don't let that stupid shit keep you from taking it. We need some color up there. Maybe we'll finally get some color in the magazine."

"Yeah, well, that's the plan. Take care, Gloria, I'll see you."

"Awright."

On the turnpike on my way to the paper the car phone rang. One of the few perks was having a car phone.

"So how'd the interview go?"

"Hi, sweetie. It was great, they made me an offer."

"Oh, that's terrific. Congratulations, sweetheart. When do you start?"

"In a few weeks. I still have to give them five more references."

"Well, that's no biggie. Is it?"

"It's not what they ask White folks, but—"

"How do you know what they usually ask—"

"A Black woman who works there told me, one of the secretaries."

"A secretary, Alice? How would she know?"

"The secretaries always know, Jack."

"Yeah, I guess you're right. Anyway, I gotta go, but let's celebrate tonight, okay? I should be home for dinner."

"Okay."

"Love you—"

I hung up and began composing my resignation speech in my head. One went like this: "Sam, I want you to know that the last five years that I've worked here have been a complete waste of time. You have no idea what you could have had in me and in the other Black reporters you have here, who you use only as translators for ghettoese. You are a racist dog and I quit."

It was so much fun imagining all the things I could finally say to him that by the time I got to the paper, I was in quite a happy mood.

•

"Hi, hon," Betty greeted me.

"Hey, Betty. Is Sam in yet?"

"Think so."

I went over to my desk and sat down at my terminal. It was still early, just before eleven, and the newsroom was not yet awake. I turned on my computer screen, more out of something to do than an effort to work. Stein was on the phone and summoned me with his finger to come up to his desk, the city desk. I wanted to give him the finger but resisted. Instead I ignored him and got up to walk to Sam Ford's office. When I got to his door it was open and he was sitting at his desk, looking at his computer screen.

"Alice, how ya doin'?" he said without glancing up. "Damn, market's down again," he said to himself. Finally he focused on me. "So what can I do for you? Have a seat, have a seat."

I unintentionally cleared my throat and leaned forward in my chair. "Yes, um, well, I've been thinking a lot about my situation here, and I was really disappointed that I didn't get the legal affairs beat—"

"Yeah, Larry told me that you were a little burnt, but Wojack just had more contacts. You shouldn't get discouraged—"

"Well, I have more experience than Wojack—"

"Well, you've got to pay your dues—"

"And when did Wojack pay his?"

"Now, Alice, your time will come."

"I've been here for five years—and I really want to do other stories, not just fires and zoning meetings—"

"And you will."

I heard myself whining and couldn't figure out why I was bothering to go through these motions. I'm outta here, I remind myself.

"I want a beat and a shot at some decent Sunday A ones," I went on.

"Well, well, you know Sunday, uh, well, that's, the vets get that. You have to be a little more patient. A beat, I don't know when we can give you that."

"I think I've been patient. I busted my butt when you had me in the sticks for a year, and I haven't been rewarded for any of that. Wojack just got here and— Look, I came in here to tell you that I've found another job and I'll be leaving in a week."

He didn't say anything for what seemed like an hour. He actually looked hurt.

"Well, if you really want to leave, Alice, I wish you the best."

"Yes, I really want to leave. I wish that things had turned out differently. When I came here I was really hopeful, but it became clear that you were not interested in having any real diverse representation. I can't be another Black reporter who becomes a piece of furniture here. It's not right that the desk automatically gives a Black reporter every call that comes in from a distressed mother whose kid is stuck in a public housing elevator. It's like we've got to do double time as social workers. It's not why I became a journalist."

"Well, Alice, I hear what you're saying, and I will give it some thought."

He turned back to his computer screen and began to call up stories to read. I took my cue, relieved to leave.

•

I FELT AS IF I'D just seen Sherman marching through Georgia when I got home from the paper. I would work through the next week, have the five additional references faxed, and take a week off before starting at *View*. I went into the bedroom to change out of my work clothes and stood in front of the full-length bedroom mirror. I was aroused just thinking about the night before with Jack. I smiled at myself and looked around the bedroom, remembering last night, when I got home and climbed into bed. I had snuggled behind Jack and awakened him. I'd kissed his back, his neck, his hair.

•

He was still drowsy when he touched my cheek with the back of his hand and told me how much he'd missed me.

"I was only gone for three days."

"And almost three nights."

With that he pulled me toward him and pushed the spaghetti strap off my shoulder. He sucked the ball of my shoulder and then ran his tongue across my chest, lightly tonguing my nipples, the way I liked. He'd learned to stop biting. I put my hands into his boxers and rubbed his groin and between his thighs. He grabbed me around my waist and pulled me toward him with a force that let me know that he really had missed me. His firmness was between my legs, under my nightgown.

"Can I put it in?" he whispered. That meant, "Is your diaphragm in?"

"Put it in."

We rocked with me on top for only a few minutes before he came. He said he was sorry, but I didn't mind.

I decided to commemorate my homecoming. I ordered a celebratory meal from Remi and put a bottle of Taittinger into the refrigerator. When he came home he found me in my orange-and-pink kimono, the table set with our best Italian dishes and linen from Portico, white beeswax candles in Nambe holders, and the Taittinger on ice.

"This is nice, but I was going to do all this." He took off his blazer.

"I'm just feeling so good."

"I'm glad."

"I'm sorry the place was such a mess when you came home. Looks like Maria came today—"

"Yeah, she did."

We sat down at the table. Our dinners were still hot on the plates.

"Jeff spent a couple nights on the couch—"

"Oh boy, are things that bad with Laura?"

"Looks like they're not gonna make it—"

"Well, I can't say that I'm surprised. At least they didn't have kids."

"I know."

"So what finally happened?"

"Well, you know, Jeff says Laura's driving him crazy. He got drunk when we went out. He's drinking too much—"

"Oh, no."

"He's really in a lotta pain. He feels like he's given her everything she asked for and she's still not happy—"

"Like the house—"

"Yeah, that house with the crazy mortgage—"

"That place is huge—"

"He's feeling used, you know."

"Well, at least his instincts are right—"

"In all the years that I've known Jeff, I've never seen him so down, not even when he almost got kicked out of med school—"

"I didn't know that. What happened?"

"Oh, I don't wanna talk about all that now. Let's make a toast. Here's to us and to staying together."

"That's nice."

We ate our watercress and endive salad, spinach ravioli, and seafood risotto.

"So tell me about what happened to Jeff in med school."

"Oh, it was some dumb shit. These guys were cheating and got kicked out and somebody said that Jeff knew about it and the school thought he should've turned them in and he had to go before the disciplinary board for not ratting on them—"

"Well, that seems ridiculous—"

"I know. Then around the same time his father, who he never really knew, had been stabbed to death by some woman in a bar . . . but even then he didn't seem as bad as he is now—"

"Poor Jeff."

I poured Jack and me champagne.

"You know, Jeff's gained about fifteen pounds. I don't know what to do—"

"What can you do? Just be his friend."

"So, what else did you do while I was gone?"

"I had a bitch of a surgery on Saturday night—"

"Saturday? Were you on call?"

"No, but I told Griffin I'd fill in for him if anything came up. You know he's getting married."

"Do I know him?"

"Yeah. I think so, I don't know. Anyway, I had a seven-hour abdominal aorta aneurysm. I didn't think the patient was gonna make it."

"Why was it so bad?"

"Four surgeons and a scrub nurse who didn't know what the hell she was doing. A couple docs made a formal complaint."

Jack never moaned about work. He loved surgery and took even the most horrendous situations in stride. I felt guilty that I hadn't been here for him over the last few months. I'd been so self-involved. I wanted to apologize but didn't want to call attention to my absence.

"Seven hours with a bad scrub nurse is hell—"

"I'm sorry."

"It's all right. It's over now."

•

"So what'd you do when you got home that night?"

"Aw, I uh—"

"Was Jeff still staying here?"

"Um, no. He'd gone home."

"So why didn't you call me at my aunt's? We could've at least talked on the phone."

"Eh, it was late. I didn't wanna bother you. You had your own stuff to deal with. By the way, how—"

"It's okay. I really am feeling better."

"Good. I'm glad, and I'm glad you're home."

•

B SMITH'S IS A bright, popular nouvelle cuisine restaurant in the theater district. Its large-windowed, high-tech exterior contrasts sharply with the surrounding cheap drugstores and porn theaters but doesn't dissuade customers from flocking. Clair Russworm was one of the faithful. She liked that it was a smartly decorated restaurant, that it was owned by an elegant Black woman, and that there was Black help, which is a suspiciously rare sight in other optimum Manhattan restaurants. She also liked to see and be seen by whatever gentry happened upon the place.

•

Mrs. Russworm was waiting when I got there. Oh shit, I thought to myself, but I looked at my watch and it was one o'clock exactly. As I walked toward the table, my black Lycra skirt was riding up and looking even shorter than it was. I was sure she made note of it, but I was feeling too high to let her get to me. I'd just finished my first eight-week tryout at *View* and was now officially a senior editor. Holly was growing on me, and I liked the work. Jack and I were getting along great, the sex was good, and we were in the process of deciding on a date and a place to get married. I was glad not to have to commute to Newark anymore, although I did miss hard news. I couldn't shake the feeling that *View,* a fashion magazine, was not exactly a conduit for societal improvement, but I didn't miss the constant musing that being in Newark, home, had caused. I wasn't fatigued. It was weird how life can seem unbearable one minute and the next one everything is gravy.

I yanked at my skirt and smiled. Clair Russworm bared her teeth at me in return.

"Have you been waiting long?"

"Oh, I wasn't waiting. I always arrive twenty minutes early. I like to just people watch."

"I see. Well, it's nice to see you."

Clair reached up and gave a perfect air kiss. "Same, dear. You look lovely. And congratulations on your job. Jack told me, senior editor. Sounds very impressive. You know, I have a subscription."

"Really, well, that's nice."

Clair was making small talk while fiddling with her ring. "Well, Alice, you know I've been wanting us to have lunch for a while now. We should get to know each other since you are marrying my Jack."

"Yes, I know, I'm sorry we haven't been able to do this sooner, but—"

•

"No need for excuses, dear, I know you're a career girl, very busy. Now how are the wedding plans? Jack tells me you're looking for a place."

"Well, sort of. Neither of us is into having a big wedding, so we're just discussing how small we want to go."

"Mmmm. A small ceremony would be nice, I suppose."

The waiter came and took the orders. Clair ordered a second martini.

"Dear, is there anything you want to ask me regarding our family or anything, maybe about Jack?" Clair said, fishing for the olive from her first drink.

"Well, I don't know. I guess I have a lot of questions. Jack doesn't talk that much about his family, other than his grandfather, whom he talks about all the time."

"Yes, Evander was very important to Jack. I guess Jack sees him more like another father than a grandfather."

"Seems that way."

Clair looked down at her hands, still twisting her large ruby ring.

"So, how did you and Jack's father meet?"

"Did I ever show you my ring?" she asked, ignoring my question. Her extended hand hung across the white linen tablecloth like a lobster's claw.

I took her hand and examined the ring. "I don't think I've ever seen it up close. It's absolutely beautiful."

It was a square-cut ruby with a round diamond on each side in an ornate antique platinum setting. She took her hand back and looked admiringly at the ring. "Yes. It had belonged to Ida Russworm, my mother-in-law. Evander, Jack's grandfather, had given it to her when they got engaged."

"That's nice. She must have thought a lot of you."

•

"Well,.people do things for all kinds of reasons, dear. She gave Clayton, Jack's father, the ring to give to me when Jack was born."

My salmon salad and her stuffed shrimp sat ignored.

"Actually, dear, my in-laws detested me. They didn't think I was good enough to marry their son."

"Really?" I was genuinely surprised.

"I was pregnant when we married. They thought I had tricked him."

"Gosh."

"For forty years of marriage they never made me feel welcomed into that family. I was always treated as an outsider, and believe me, it took its toll on our marriage."

"Did you ever confront them?"

"Oh, many times, and they would say I was as much a part of the family as Clayton was."

"But why do you think they didn't like you?"

"They were from old money, an old Black family, and frankly, the Russworms were snobs. I came from a poor family, and I was the first person in my family to go to college."

"Jack hasn't painted that kind of picture of them, as snobs."

"Well, dear, perhaps you haven't noticed, but our Jack is a snob. He's my only child, he's a wonderful person, but he's one of them."

She had had a few gin martinis.

"Well, Mrs. Russworm—"

"Call me Clair, dear."

"Clair, I have to tell you that I don't see that in Jack."

"He's contrary, his grandfather was that way. He's also very naive."

"He's never talked about him like that."

•

"I know, he probably doesn't remember that."

"What about your family?"

"We were pretty removed from my family. I'd disowned them when I married Clayton."

"Are you still estranged?"

"My sister and I have been talking again lately, and you know, that's in part because of you."

"Me?"

"When I met you, you reminded me of me when I was young, feeling insecure but trying so hard to make the right impression. But you're proud of where you come from."

"Well, I've had my moments, too, hiding things."

"I'd been estranged from my family for years and years, and I just recently picked up the phone and called my sister. We've been getting together for dinner and lunch—"

"That's great."

"You know, I'm glad Jack is marrying someone like you. Had he married Sherry, I would've been happy, I liked her, but things for me would've continued the way they were. I wouldn't have ever talked to her the way I did with you today."

The last of the lunch crowd had gone and the staff was setting the tables for dinner. I sat across from Clair Russworm, looking into her powdered face, trying to determine whether this was someone I could trust.

On my way back to the office, I picked up the *Post* to check out page six for model gossip. When I got back to the office there were seven messages, one from Jack, the rest from publicists. I sat down, dialed Jack, put on the speakerphone, and leafed through the paper. A small item in the bottom left corner caught my eye.

A lung specialist in Westchester County's posh Pelham Estates has been charged with aggravated assault for allegedly attacking his wife with a baseball bat in the couple's home last night.

It couldn't be, I told myself. I jumped when I heard Jack's voice through the speakerphone.

"Hi, have you talked to Jeff today?" I picked up the receiver.

"No, why?"

"Uh, it's probably nothing. It's just, um, this item in the *Post* I was just reading when you came through, um, I'm sure it's nothing."

"Well, what is it?"

"It's just this doctor in Pelham Estates that's been arrested for beating his wife—"

"Alice, do you know how many doctors there must be in Pelham Estates?"

"Well, yeah, I'm sure you're right, but the guy is a lung specialist."

"Yeah, well, Jeff probably knows him."

"Yeah, of course, it's not Jeff."

"So, how'd lunch go with my mom?"

"Fine, good, actually."

"Well, tell me all about it later. I've gotta laparoscopy scheduled in a few minutes. I'll be home for dinner, okay?"

"Okay."

"I love you, Alice."

"Me too."

Jack was sitting on the couch, his back facing me, having a Glenfiddich, when I got home. He jumped when he heard the jangle of my keys dropping onto the glass foyer table.

"Hey," I said.

"Hi. How you doin'?"

I quickly sorted through the mail that had been lying on the table and dropped my suede sack to the floor before kissing Jack on the mouth. I handed him a folded copy of the *New York Post* opened to the story about the lung doctor beating his wife.

"What's this for?"

"Read it."

"What? Alice—"

"Have you heard from Jeff yet?"

"No."

"You tried to reach him?"

"Yeah."

"And he hasn't answered his beeper, right?"

"Right, but—"

"Isn't it highly unusual for a doctor not to answer his beeper?"

"Yeah, but Alice, come on. Jeff wouldn't—I think you've written too many police stories."

He opened the tabloid and read.

"I just have this weird feeling," I said.

He finished reading and looked at me. "You know, you are so pretty and bronzed."

"Bronzed?"

"Yeah, your skin, that's what it looks like."

"Thanks. So what do you think?"

"It's just a coincidence."

"You really think there could be more than one lung specialist living on Fox Run Drive?"

"It's possible."

"Jack—"

"Beating her? That couldn't be Jeff."

•

"I hope you're right," I said, standing in the middle of the living room, trying to find something to do to occupy myself.

The phone rang and I snapped it up. Jack looked at me with his chin resting on his palm.

"Alice, it's Mrs. . . . Clair."

"Hi, Clair, how are you?"

"I'm fine, dear. Is Jack at home yet?"

"Yeah. He's right here. I'll put him on."

"Hi, Mom. How're you? . . . I'm okay. . . . What are you talking about? . . . Heard what? . . . Well, no, I haven't heard anything, I've beeped him, but he isn't responding to his beeper. Beyond that . . . She's right here with me, why?"

Jack stood up and sat back down again. The blood rushed from his face. "Mother, I don't need a drink—what have you heard? . . . No, tell me what you know for a fact, not some gossip."

He ran his hand over his head and let out a gush of air. He inhaled again, deeply, and closed his eyes as his mother told him what she knew. She told him it was true, that Jeffrey had admitted to hitting Laura. An attorney who was at Clair's cocktail party for Jeff had been called. The attorney's wife, a club member of Clair's, called her with the news. Jack was silent. I took the receiver from his hand.

"Hello, Mrs. Russworm, Clair. Do you know something?"

"Yes, dear. It's true. Ray Black's wife, Harriette, called to tell me."

"So where is he now?"

"In the Westchester County Jail. What's Jack doing?"

"He's sitting on the couch, right here next to me. He isn't up to this right—"

"Why don't you fix him a Scotch, dear. I think we should all go up there. I'm coming down there."

"Yes, I will."

•

I hung up and sat down next to Jack and gathered him in my arms. "Your mother's coming down so we can all go to Westchester. Is that all right?"

"I don't want to go up there now. Did my mother say that he admitted to doing it?"

"Yes, that's what she said."

Jeff was brought to the visitors' booth wearing orange overalls. His face looked ashy and gray. His body language was still confident, but different. It was more of a street pose, from his Brooklyn days.

"Yo, my man Jack, whazzup?" Jeff said over the small Plexiglas partition that separated him from us. I sat next to Jack. Clair waited outside.

I had to fight back tears. Jack didn't bother.

"Jeff, man, damn, what . . . ?"

Jack held his head down.

"I know, this is fucked up, huh? Not exactly part of the game plan," Jeff said.

I understood that Jeff had on his hard stance because in a place like this, it was survival. I wasn't sure Jack understood this.

"Listen, do you need me to do anything? You need money?" Jack asked.

"Naw, I'm all right. Black is workin' at gettin' bail set, gettin' me outta here. I'll be outta here by tomorrow."

"Jeff, man, what happened?"

"I guess somethin' in me just snapped. You know. Like Laura, you know, man, she knew how to get to me. She knew my buttons and she just pushed them. I just couldn't take her anymore."

"But, Jeff, a baseball bat?"

"I don't even have a bat. The local rag reported that and all the papers just picked the shit up. I hit her once, with my hand."

•

"Well . . . that's good. I mean, that it wasn't a bat."

"I know it's still fucked up, but she just wouldn't stop, man, she was talking to me like I was garbage, talking about my family and shit. I had to make her stop. You know what? She wasn't shit. Wit all her knowin' about art and speakin' French, she was lower than any of the women I knew from the projects."

Jack slouched at the table, his head held down, not looking Jeff in the eye.

Jeff continued. "Man, I hope you know what you got in Alice." He nodded toward me, and I smiled awkwardly. "Now, she's a jewel, man. Y'all should be married already. Don't fuck up."

"Yeah, Alice is . . . well, at least you got Ray Black, he's one of the best. My father was always talking about how bad Black was, that he could get Jack the Ripper off."

We all laughed.

"Well, I ain't no Jack the Ripper, but my ass is goin' before the ethics board for this one."

As if on cue, a guard with arms the size of fireplugs tapped Jeff's chair. "Time's up, doc."

"Okay, man," Jeff said to the guard, then turned back to us. "Yo, Jack, man, thanks for comin' up. I'll see y'all later. Don't worry about me. Bye, Alice."

"I'm gonna worry about you. I'll see you at the hearing."

"Awright."

We sat and watched Jeff. As he was being escorted back to his cell, he chatted with the guard as if he were at a cocktail party instead of jail. He waved to us as he headed toward his unit in protective custody, a privilege enjoyed by people like him, the person he'd become. A place where the system kept professionals apart from the criminal masses.

•

I KNEW JACK WAS really hurting because of Jeff. The situation was beyond anything that he had ever had to deal with. Wife abuse. Jail. Court. People like Jack had only a *tsk-tsk*ing relationship with the kinds of people who found themselves before a judge. I, on the other hand, had personally known plenty of people who had been in jail, out, and back again. Abdul had done seven years for armed robbery, which was how he'd found Islam. Before Abdul, there were the thuggy boys in my neighborhood who were in and out for petty things like car theft. Duke, one of the more desired ones back in the day, had increased his rap sheet with each birthday, and by the time he reached twenty-one, he was doing life for murdering a gas station attendant during an attempted armed robbery.

Once when I was working at the paper and assigned to cover city hall in Newark, I was given a tour of the police headquarters. The sergeant took me to see the holding cells in the basement. While we were there, someone called out my name from behind bars. I turned around, trying to figure out who the hell would know me down here. I walked over, double-strand pearls draped across my silk shirt and swinging from side to side, and got right up to the bars to get a good look.

"Sidney? Is that you?"

"Yeah, girl, it's *moi,*" said my childhood best friend.

"Sidney, what are you doing in there?"

Sidney had been a drag queen for more than a decade now, supporting himself or herself primarily through petty thefts like selling pills, mostly amphetamines.

The sergeant stood nearby and looked at his shoes.

"Well, what are you in here for?"

"Girl, don't even ask. Some trumped-up bullshit they got me on, but my attorney is workin' on it. I'll be out before nighttime."

I was stumped for something to say, but I didn't want Sidney to know that. "So, how's your mutha doin'?"

"She's fine." He brightened. "So what you doin' now? I hear you kinda livin' large."

It was the kind of comment that people from the old neighborhood made all the time, that felt to me like an ice bath in January. I never knew how to respond. Many times it was from someone who didn't like me and I didn't give a shit about. Sidney was someone from my painful childhood years who had been a comfort to me and he was genuinely happy for whatever success he thought I'd achieved, but I felt guilty, as if I'd survived some horrible war that had claimed him. To stave off some of these feelings I adopted his vernacular, which used to be ours—like saying "mutha" for mother. What used to be our shared tongue, our way of communicating, when we lived on the same block, when we were part of the same tribe, now seemed almost as foreign as the language my ancestors spoke in the motherland. There was comfort in that tribe, but I had had to learn another language, the language of the larger world, in order to move on, what was supposed to be ahead. Sometimes, though, I wondered if my moody periods, my blues, weren't for the things I'd left behind or was it simply confirmation that while I was from the block I was never of it. At times like these I missed Miles. He and I at least shared a similar journey. Of course, there were things about him that I didn't like. His near obsession with style over substance—being at whatever the new hot restaurant was the minute it opened and never going back once it was no longer de rigueur. I also hated that, the way he'd sprinkle his conversation with French phrases. Even more I also hated that he said "ciao." Early in our romance I overlooked *ciao*.

I tried to take the attention off me and put it back on Sidney. "So, you still sketchin' and sewin'?"

"Girl, please. I ain't sewed shit in so long—"

He'd been a wonderful seamstress and used to dream of becoming a designer. I felt an ache in my chest, and all I wanted to do was get away. We promised to stay in touch. I handed him my business card through the bars, after checking with the cop to make sure it was okay. I had scribbled my home number on the back and prayed that he wouldn't use it.

"Yeah, girl, we need to stay in touch."

"I know."

He never called.

•

• • •

On the day of Jeff's arraignment, we all piled into my Saab. Jack drove, I sat in the front seat, and his mother and Jeff's mother were in the back. The only one who spoke was Jeff's mother, and she talked practically the entire way to White Plains, about a forty-five-minute drive from Manhattan.

"Jeffrey's always been a good boy. Don't know how he could've let hisself get in this kinda mess. Who'd a thought it? Such a good boy, as I live and breathe. Ump, ump ump . . . I wonder what dey gone set bail at?"

"Don't worry about money, Mrs. Doran, I can take care of it," Jack said, looking at her through the rearview mirror.

"Poor Jeffrey. I know he feel so bad being up there in all this mess. He was always a good boy, used to mine me when none of them girls I got would. He's always been a joy, always made me real proud. He was always makin' plans. Used to say, 'Mama, I'm gonna make somethin' outta myself.' I knew he'd be somethin', but I never dreamed he'd be a doctor, though."

I understood she was nervous and upset. She didn't really know any of us, she'd only met me and Mrs. Russworm at the wedding, an event I was sure she wished had never happened.

The Westchester County Courthouse is a majestic limestone structure that sits in the center of White Plains, the county seat. The attorney, Ray Black, a sixtysomething fox with a salt-and-pepper afro and mustache, was huddled, whispering with Jeff, at the defendant's table. I realized that this was the first time I had ever seen Jeff and Laura apart. She was nowhere around, but her parents had come up from D.C. to be in the courtroom and were sitting with an attractive woman I didn't know.

The judge granted Jeff bail of $50,000. Jack got up to post it immediately after hearing the judgment. The young woman with Laura's parents followed him.

"Well, I'm glad that part is settled. Jeffrey shouldn't have to spend one minute more in jail with those animals," Clair said.

I smiled at her and kept silent, trying to figure out who the woman who followed Jack was.

"So, dear, how're the wedding plans going?"

"Um, okay. We've settled on sometime in late spring, early summer."

"Wonderful," Clair said, and clasped her hands together. "What do you need me to do?"

"Um, nothing, yet. I'll let you know."

"Good. Don't hesitate, now."

•

THE LATE WINTER usually brought some serious melancholy, but this time I was as sunny as a tour guide in Tobago. Jack and I had set a date for Memorial Day weekend, and I'd found the perfect gallery to have the wedding and hired one of the graphic artists at the magazine to design the invitations at cost, and one of the fashion photogs was going to shoot it as a gift. Things with Jeff had basically worked out. Seemed his lawyer got the charges reduced to a lesser assault offense, since he hadn't used a bat. Jeff went before the ethics board and received, as a slap on the hand, three months of shrinkage, which seemed to really help him sort out a comfortable arrangement with his demons. He bought a co-op in a friendly part of Prospect Park and seemed to be happy. He seemed to even be having a positive effect on Jack, who wasn't the most introspective person. Laura had moved back to D.C., and we heard she was dating a dermatologist.

I got home from work and took out chicken breasts to defrost in the microwave for dinner. I played the answering machine that sat on the kitchen counter. The tape made a whirring sound as it rewound messages.

"Hi, it's me. I might be late at the hospital. I'll call you later. Bye." *Beep.*

I pushed Cancel on the microwave and put the chicken back in the refrigerator.

"Hi, Alice, this is Sherry, Sherry Steptoe. I don't know if you know me, but Jack and I used to be, um, we used to date. Alice, would you give me a call, please? My number is five four oh—" *Click.* "Oh, um, there's my other line. Um, Alice, I'll call you back. Bye." *Beep.*

Sherry Steptoe? What could she want with me? The phone rang and interrupted my thoughts.

"Hullo."

"Hi," Jack said, sounding distracted.

"How're you?"

"Oh, I'm all right. Just came out of an emergency appendectomy and the guy's not doing too hot. I'm gonna hang around in case something happens."

"Are you all right?"

"Yeah. How was your day?"

"Great. I found a place for us to have the wedding."

"Oh yeah? Where?"

"It's in SoHo, on West Broadway, and it's perfect."

"Sounds good."

"It is. When can you come with me to see it?"

"I don't know, sweetie. This week doesn't look good. But go ahead and reserve it. I trust your taste."

"Jack, that's not the point. I want you to see it."

"Okay, okay. How 'bout, um, next Tuesday?"

"Fine. Listen, do you have a minute?"

"Yeah. What's the matter?"

"I got a weird call today."

"Oh yeah? From?" Jack was interrupted by a resident and began giving instructions to increase a patient's medication. "I'm sorry. You were saying?"

"I got a weird call."

"Uh-huh. From?"

"From Sherry Steptoe."

"Sherry? What'd she say?"

"Uh, nothing. She left a message, and then someone was trying to get through on her other line so she didn't leave the number. Do you have one for her?"

"Um, probably, somewhere. Listen, sweetie, things are getting a little hairy here, I've gotta go, okay? Bye."

Jack hung up before I could say good-bye. I put the cordless on the counter and pulled out a drawer to look for take-out menus. While I was waiting for my moo shu chicken to arrive, I couldn't stop thinking about why Sherry Steptoe was calling me. I called Cheryl.

"Well, why would she be calling you?"

"I don't know, genius, that's why I'm asking you."

"Hmmm. It's a strange one. Do you think it has something to do with your wedding? Maybe she's got something to tell you about—"

"Well, of course I think it has something to do with us getting married. The question is what."

"Mmmm. Girlfriend, I wanna be on a three-way when you do talk to Miss Thang."

"Cheryl, this is serious. I'm really worried."

"Alice, it's probably nothing. She may wanna buy you a gift and wants to know where you're registered."

"Oh, come on. He practically left her at the altar—"

"'Scuse me, Miss Girl, practically all that was missin' was the veil."

We both laughed, but mine was counterfeit. I didn't find the image of a woman waiting at the altar for her intended or getting blown off the night before the wedding even remotely humorous. Cheryl thought it was a riot.

"Well, look," she said after she'd regained herself, "why don't you just call information, get her number, and find out what the ho wants?"

"You don't think that I'd seem too anxious?"

"Who cares? You are anxious, and you don't have to worry about how you seem to her."

"You're right—"

"As always—"

"Oh, shut up. Listen, my food's here."

"Yeah, I should get back to work."

The lobby of Young & Rubicam belies its power. The small entrance is tucked discreetly into Madison Avenue in the mid-Forties. A narrow double door is sided by two revolving doors. To the right is a slim podium and a guard; to the left is a newspaper stand that sells candy, magazines, cigarettes, and such. For a company of such bulk, a company that is one of the foremost advertising powerhouses in the country, responsible for selling brand-name products to most of the free world, there's no marble or waterfall or expensive artwork that graces most other powerful Manhattan corporate lobbies.

I got into the elevator and hit nine. I had taken half the day off to check out florists and reserve the gallery. Jack hadn't been able to go with me, and I was afraid we would lose our date. I was disappointed, but when planning a wedding, the mind is able to block out all kinds of small annoyances. You're the equivalent of a navy SEAL on a seek-and-destroy mission. It requires nerves and focus. When I got off the elevator, there was no receptionist, just numbers and arrows directing me. I stopped for a moment to remember the number of the office and turned right. When I got there Sherry was sitting on a high swivel chair with her back to the door. She looked as if she were staring out of the window onto Madison. The office was smallish and modern and had a drafting table that took up most of the space and a teak bookcase against a wall. On one of the shelves was a small silver framed picture of Sherry and Jack with some older people at what looked like a picnic. I knocked on the opened door.

She spun her body around in her chair. "You must be Alice?"

I nodded.

"Did you have any problems finding the office?"

"Not at all, your directions were perfect." I stood in the middle of the room, my shoulder bag slung across my body. I recognized her face from court, at Jeff's arraignment. She was the woman who'd followed Jack. I was bothered by the picture—why would she still display a picture of him?—but even more, I felt panic in my stomach once I'd placed her face.

•

"I spend a lot of time just looking out the window. I tell myself that I'm being creative," she said, now fiddling with the latch on her gold watch, obviously trying to break the tension.

She was wearing tan wide-legged trousers that matched the wool gabardine jacket, which she wore with a blue silk crewneck underneath. She wore a simple gold watch and gold disk earrings. Her makeup was obvious, and her thick reddish hair was long and heavy. It was parted on one side and hung dramatically over her face like Veronica Lake. I envied her hair.

"So did you want to talk here?" I said, reminding her that this was not a social call.

"Oh, no. I was hoping we could go for a coffee, maybe have a little lunch. Is your time okay?"

"Yeah, that's fine. We can do that."

My curiosity was boiling over. I had talked to her over the phone the day before, and she had called back after I'd worried a hole in my stomach and insisted we get together in person to talk. I hadn't had a chance to talk to Jack because he had come in late and gone out early this morning.

Sherry and I walked a few blocks from her office to a nondescript coffee shop, the kind that appears on every other corner in Manhattan. What a strange skin I felt myself in, sitting across from Sherry. I looked good in my black quilted anorak, jeans, zippered, black leather vest over a white T-shirt, but for a moment I was back at college, looking at Sherry, remembering how girls like her used to make me feel ashamed of my working-class background. Back then I longed for a family background like Sherry's.

Sherry had gone to Wellesley and I, only a few miles away, to Mount Holyoke, but after a few attempts at Negro Geography, it became obvious that we ran in different crowds. I had been a scholarship student that society was going to uplift because I showed promise. Sherry surely had been a regular admit. I imagined her driving off to school in a new convertible Fiat spider and a fleet of Louis Vuitton luggage that Mummy and Daddy had given her as going-away presents stacked behind her. I could just picture them waving her off, standing in the circular driveway in front of their Greek Revival. My trip to college, a stark contrast, was made in my parents' old Buick with discarded brown lunch bags on the back-seat. On the way to South Hadley that day, I'd told myself that I didn't have promise. I just wanted to be back on Fenton Avenue with the new neighborhood toughs chasing me home, making me feel like somebody, even if it was somebody they hated. I was about to be just another Black girl who'd made it through, a survivor. I had spent my childhood trying to be gritty, feeling guilty about my clothes, my piano lessons, and my pretty bedroom, and now I was supposed to do an about-face and do *Gidget Goes to College*.

Sherry had the comportment that I'd erroneously thought all the doctors' and lawyers' daughters had: the neat, wrinkle-free clothes, perfect little Pappagallo-type shoes, and jewelry that was never intrusive, never loud.

"See anything interesting?" Sherry said from behind the over-size coffee shop menu.

"Um, yeah, I'm just going to have soup." Split pea. I didn't have an appetite.

"Okay, I see what I want." She motioned for the waitress, who came and took our orders.

Sherry turned her attention to me. Her light, casual way was gone. "Alice, I know this must seem strange, me calling you out of the blue and wanting to talk," she said, playing with her silver-ware.

"Yeah, I have to say, I'm more than a little curious."

"Well, I don't know how to begin." She sighed. "I will say that I had hoped to avoid this, but—"

"Sherry, um, you can just say whatever it is—" I took a gulp of water from the diner-issue brown glass.

"Well, Jack and I—" She was moving her hands.

I felt hot and shifted in my seat. We were momentarily distracted by the waitress, who delivered my soup and Sherry's burger platter. Sherry looked down at her plate as if deciding what to do with the greasy slab that was leaking oil and blood onto the white bun. I didn't take my eyes off her.

"You and Jack what?" I heard myself sounding petulant.

"I'm sorry to have to tell you this. I gave Jack time to tell you, and he didn't, so, well, Jack and I slept together two months ago and I'm pregnant."

I heard the words "slept together" and "pregnant" but could focus only on the fucking aspect. It was too much info to process at once. That Jack had cheated on me was one piece, with Sherry, of all people, was another, and she was pregnant? I couldn't think of what to say, how to react. An image of Jack's body going up and coming down onto Sherry's flashed in my head. I pictured him being too swept away to use a condom. People didn't just get pregnant by accident these days. I couldn't believe that she was sitting in front of me telling me this.

"So, what, you decide to invite me to lunch to tell me that you're pregnant by my fiancé? What the fuck do you expect me to say, congratulations? I mean, what kinda fuckin' game is this? This is bullshit, Sherry. This is bullshit, okay, and I don't want to hear this shit from you. What did you expect me to say—"

"Alice, look, I can understand you being upset, but that's not why—" Her eyes were pleading, and her hands were clutching the table's edge.

"Oh, fuck that, you most certainly fuckin' did intend to upset me, okay, or you wouldn't have told me this shit, so don't pull this innocent shit with me. Look, it seems to me that you've got a problem and you gotta work it out."

I got up from the table. The back of my T-shirt was wet with sweat. I wanted to get out of the restaurant before I started screaming and created a bigger scene. I wanted to grab her hair and wrap it around my fist until she screamed. Instead I pushed my soup bowl across the table and watched the green mush ooze into the lap of her nice gabardine.

I walked out, walking fast for thirty blocks before paying attention to where I was. I saw the Ralph Lauren store, which stands, to me, like the Confederate flag over East Seventy-second. *Welcome to the world of tradition, to the past, when everything was simple, before the Negroes had any rights.* And all this from a boy from the Bronx. It made me want to vomit. I wanted off the East Side as fast as possible; its serene streets and stick people were inhospitable to my rage. I felt betrayed, surely, but I also sensed this weird feeling of relief, like when you're finally told the end of a story, like when the other shoe drops.

•

I WALKED OVER TO Fifth, then up to Mount Sinai. I called Jack's office from a phone in the lobby. A resident told me that he'd gone home for the day. I could confront him at home, but I wasn't sure I wanted to do that. His office would have forced me to be restrained, which was what I needed. I couldn't be sure what I might do in private.

Tiny pellets began falling, but I barely noticed it. I was preoccupied with trying to decide whether to go home and confront Jack or never go home again. I didn't know what to say, where to start. I needed to prepare myself for the possibilities. What if he wanted to be with Sherry? Where would that leave me? Would I try to fight for him or just let him go? I hailed a cab.

"Eighty-fifth and Madison," I said, and leaned back into the seat, my jeans wet around my ankles. The driver was listening to WNEW, a standard station. Nancy Wilson was blowing "Bewitched, Bothered and Bewildered," a song I loved. It reminded me of going to the Carlyle to see Bobby Short with Miles during our wild off-and-on days, when I'd go out with him without underwear and we'd fool around in restaurants.

I leaned up and got the driver's attention. "Would you take me to Forty-eighth and Third instead? Thanks." I sat back.

The Wang building on Third Avenue was a funny rust-colored polished stone structure that took up the entire block. Miles's office was on the thirty-fifth floor. I handed the driver a five and got out.

"Miss Andrews, how nice to see you," Gwen, Miles's secretary, said upon seeing me exit the elevator. She offered to take me to Miles's office, but I told her he wasn't expecting me.

"Oh, I'm sure he'll be glad to see you, just go right in," she said. Secretaries always know where the bodies are buried.

Miles was walking back and forth in front of his huge picture window, talking on the headset. He looked at me, raised his eyebrows to register shock, and pointed to one of the two leather wingback chairs facing his desk.

"Yeah, yeah, I know that's what was said, but that was last year, Bob. This is a whole new deal, man, with a less profitable company. . . . Yeah, well, you talk it over with your guys and get back to me. . . . Yeah. You bet. I'm here, ready to rock and roll. . . . Okay, buddy. You bet."

His conversation ended, he took off the mouthpiece and turned his attention to me.

"Alice Andrews, well, how the hell are you, and to what do I owe this magnificent surprise?" Miles could have been a Baptist preacher. He was dressed impeccably in a blue shirt, white collar, loud tie, and black-and-gold suspenders holding up his charcoal cuffed trousers. He was still standing and looking at me from behind his desk.

"I was in the neighborhood," I said sheepishly.

"Uh-huh—so what's up, babe? How ya been? How're the wedding plans going?" he said, coming from behind his desk.

"Everything is fine, you know, I mean, we're not having a big wedding, so there are no real plans—"

"Hmmmm, and how's Doctor Wonderful?"

"Jack is, um, okay."

"So what are you doing here?" Miles said, reverting back to the no bullshit tone he had been using during his phone call.

"Really, I was in a cab and I heard a song that reminded me of you and going to the Carlyle to hear Bobby Short and I just thought I'd stop by and say hi, but I know you're busy so I'll go—"

"Whoa. Sit down, relax. You want tea or somethin'? Coffee, juice?" Sticking out his fingers as if he were a catcher giving the pitcher cues.

"No thanks."

Miles was 90 percent asshole, but the 10 percent of him that was sweet was really sweet and sensitive. He knew something was wrong, and when he showed me his tender side I always felt close to him. Tears flooded my eyes.

He walked across the thick deep green carpet to close his office door. He pulled the matching wingback chair close to me and put his hands on mine. "What is it, baby? What's the matter?"

His concern made me cry harder. He handed me his monogrammed linen handkerchief and pulled my head into his well-developed chest.

•

"I just had lunch with Jack's old girlfriend," I said between sobs, "and she's pregnant—by him!"

Miles just rubbed my head and searched for something to say. His instinct would lead him to say something sarcastic, but his basic humanity would tell him not to.

"Oh, baby, I'm so sorry. What can I do?"

"Just stay like this for a while," I said, sniffing. I just needed to feel something familiar.

Miles held me until my face and his shirt were wet. "Listen, let me get you some tea, okay?" He gently pushed me back, holding on to my shoulders at his arm's length.

I sniffed.

Usually he would've had Gwen bring whatever he wanted, but he went to fetch the tea himself. When we were dating I used to love to raid his company's kitchen late at night after we'd gone out for a movie and he had to go back to work. Sometimes we'd make love on the floor and then pig out on my favorite Pepperidge Farm Milanos and Kathleen's oatmeal cookies, kiwi and mangoes, SmartFood popcorn, Pellegrino, and Cappio. Miles came back with some cookies and a mug of Earl Grey with lemon.

He could be great when he wanted to be, which unfortunately wasn't often enough. I knew Miles was thinking that Jack was a plebeian for fucking someone on the side and getting caught like this. It wasn't something that he would have ever allowed to happen to him. Smugness was as much a part of Miles as his suspenders, but I was wallowing in his kindness. I took a sip of tea. Miles was munching on a cookie. We were watching each other.

"So, what you gonna do?" he said, chewing with his mouth open.

"I don't know. I haven't decided how to handle it. I'm not ready to go home and confront him yet. I guess that's why I came here."

•

"Oh, so I'm just a stopgap, huh? That's all right, baby, you can use me till you use me up. I told you before, I'll always be here for you."

"I'm not using you. Well, maybe I am. My therapist is away for a week. But I wanted to talk to you. . . ."

"Well, I guess that's a compliment. I'd better grab it. So if I'm so great, why'd you blow me off in the first place?"

It was one of those questions that couldn't be answered, and he didn't expect one. He just needed, I guess, to tell me that he still considered our breakup to be my doing. It was true that I'd actually said the words, but his behavior was why we broke up, why I was finally able to mouth the words "It's over." Our problems were numerous, but there were three that I finally decided I couldn't live with—he was a committed workaholic, whenever we did do things socially it was always what he wanted with his friends or business associates, and he was a serious hound. Even with all that, I probably would've stayed with him if he'd been making any movement toward a future together, which he was not. I never met his mother, he never wanted to meet my parents; he wouldn't give me keys to his place; and he wouldn't even talk about marriage. When I would bring it up, he'd just say he liked things the way they were.

"I guess what you need is a strategy," he said. "You've got to figure out what you want. If you wanna stay with Jack, you got to play this thing cool, tell him you need a couple of days alone to think, make him squirm. If you don't give a shit, then cuss him out, just say fuck the shit, and move on. Come back to me." His Tennessee accent was in full flourish.

"Yeah. I wish I could just sleep on it a couple days, but as it is I've got to face him."

•

"See, I told you that living together shit was not the way to go," he said, his usual self showing.

"Miles, I don't need to hear that now, okay?"

"Yeah, I know, baby."

"I did hold on to my apartment—"

"Thatta girl—"

I sighed. "I'm gonna go. Thanks for listening and for the tea. At least your shirt is dry now."

"Yeah, it's nice and crunchy now. Listen, it'll be all right. Whatever happens, it'll be all right, okay? You can always come back here. Gimme a hug."

I stood up and faced him. His arms, extending from his wide chest and taut waist, beckoned. I knew I shouldn't hug him, it would only make me want him, but I couldn't think of a good enough reason at the moment not to. Jack had cheated on me. Miles held me, our cheeks touching, he smelled like citrus, and I was getting turned on. I wrapped my arms around his lower waist. His hard body always made me horny, as did the idea of carrying on this way during business hours.

"You wanna get a room? The Four Seasons is close," he whispered.

He knew that I loved the place.

"We could have dinner . . . room service," he went on.

My favorite thing.

"You could get a massage."

My other favorite thing.

I deserved that and more, I told myself as I allowed him to press his pelvis closer.

"We could leave now."

How could I say yes? I had other things to tend to, like my life with Jack. How could I even consider what Miles was proposing? How could I say no?

I had no feeling, other than the ache between my legs. I was so hot for Miles; my sexual reaction to him hadn't changed at all. We got to the hotel, and our room was one that we'd had before. Miles called and ordered lobsters, strawberries, and champagne. He also asked for a masseur. I stood at the window overlooking Fifty-seventh Street. After he got off the phone, Miles took off his tie and unbuttoned his shirt. He pulled me toward him and kissed me hard, his tongue more frantic than I remembered. I opened my mouth and tried to push the day's events out of my mind. Miles pushed my hair back from my forehead, grabbing my face by the cheeks and kissing me on my throat.

"Damn, baby, I missed you," he whispered into my ear, trying to sound sincere.

I was silent. I realized that we'd never really had foreplay. It was always just a little grinding before we were ripping off our clothes. His attempt at foreplay was too forceful and impatient. He wanted to be inside me now. I wanted that, too, but something outside of me was telling me not to. The thought of the massage sweetened the deal, made it something I didn't want to walk away from.

A light knock let us know room service had delivered.

"Here, baby, lobster and champagne on Pratesi sheets." Miles grinned.

"Miles, I'm sorry," I whispered to him as he stuck his tongue in my ear.

"What?"

"I can't do this. I have to go."

"Yes, you can. You know you want to."

"I do, but I've gotta deal with Jack, now."

•

He pulled my arms around his waist. He was so cocky, it hurt. "No one has to know about this. It's between us, baby." He licked my neck, behind my ear, nibbled the lobe. "I really do love you, Alice. I just didn't know how to show it."

I didn't want to hear about love; I knew Miles didn't have a clue. He unzipped my leather vest and ran his hands over the thin cotton T-shirt covering my erect nipples.

"I really can't do this," I said as I let my pelvis rub his.

"Oh, baby, I've missed this."

"Please, Miles, you have to stop."

"What?"

"I can't do this. I have to go."

"What, you gotta be kiddin'."

"No, really, I can't do this. I'm sorry."

I pulled away from him, grabbed my jacket and bag, and left him standing in the middle of the floor, trying not to look pissed.

"Call me later if you need to talk. I'll be at the office," he said to my back.

The apartment was dark and quiet when I got home. Jack's brown suede Cole-Haan loafers were on the living room floor, under the coffee table, where the whiskey decanter sat next to an empty highball glass. I went in the bedroom and found Jack asleep, wrapped up in the comforter on top of the sheets.

"Hi," he said from under the cover.

His greeting was hollow. I knew that he knew I knew.

"Hi," I said back. "You pulled an all-nighter last night?"

"Just about. I came in at about three and had to be back at seven."

He sighed and rolled up to sit on the edge of the bed. He was wearing a gray Harvard T-shirt and Jockey shorts. He got up and walked to the corner grandma chair and picked up his jeans and pulled them on. He sat down and ran a hand over his thick dark curls. He looked at me. I was standing, facing him, feeling like I would overheat.

"So, where ya been?" he began.

"Where've I been?" I shouted. "Well, let's see. First I went to SoHo to reserve the gallery for our wedding," I said sarcastically.

"Listen, um, Alice, I know we've gotta talk, I just don't know what to say."

I was silent.

"Sherry called and told me about lunch. Alice, I'm so sorry, I know that's lame, but—"

"Yeah, Jack, it's very fucking lame. I'm sure you're sorry, but that doesn't mean shit to me now, okay? I just wanna know what the fuck you were doing. I mean, you had Sherry, you didn't want her, you stood her up at the damn altar. Now you find her so fuckin' irresistible that you gotta go fuck her up against a wall someplace. It's so hot now, you can't even stop to put on a goddamn rubber. What is wrong with you? Suppose she has something? And now you've passed it on to me. You fucking asshole. All over some pussy and some already had pussy at that. I swear, Jack, I can't believe you did this. You hardly fuck me without a rubber and never without birth control, and we're supposed to be gettin' married. What is this shit? Did you wanna get her pregnant? Did you wanna leave me at the altar, too? Is that your game? Well, you know you could've done that without getting her pregnant. If you didn't want me, all you had to do was say so and I'da been outta here. How could you, Jack? How could you?"

I sat down on the bed, breathing heavily, my side facing him. He got up and walked over and put his hand on my back.

"I'm so sorry, sweetheart, I never meant to hurt you. Please be-

•

lieve that. I would die first. It was just something that happened, once, it didn't mean anything. I didn't plan it, Sherry doesn't mean anything, it was just one of those things that happened. It has nothing to do with us and how I feel about you. You know I love you more than anything. You know that, don't you?"

The intensity was unlike him.

"How could you sleep with Sherry?"

"I didn't plan to do it. I went over there for some dinner—"

"Oh, and your dick just fell into her vagina—"

"Alice, I know this is bad, but I really didn't mean to do it—"

"So she seduced you—"

"Absolutely. I was stupid and naive, but I didn't plan it, you've got to believe me."

"And you did it without a rubber—"

"Yeah, you know that I don't do that—"

"And what about AIDS, did that cross your mind, Jack?"

"I know that she's a regular blood donor. I trusted her."

"And so fucking what? Did you see when she last gave blood? Did you see a donor card?"

"No."

"So you actually talked about doing it before you fucked?"

"No, no. I remembered that she was a blood donor."

"So she encouraged you to do it without any protection and you assumed she was using something?"

"Yeah, she used to be on the pill. I assumed she still was."

"Uh-huh."

"She planned the whole thing. She told me that when she told me she was pregnant. She said she'd have the baby with or without me."

"Uh-huh, and you were just carrying this around with you. When were you planning to tell me?"

"I was going to tell you. She was threatening me, trying to force my hand, and I just wasn't going to give in to her threats. I'm really sorry, sweetheart, I wanted to tell you myself, honest. I'll do anything you want me to."

"Well, why did you go to have dinner with her?"

"I don't know. I was angry at you—"

"Why?"

"For leaving—"

"Jack, I didn't leave you."

"I realize that now, but at the time—"

"At the time what?"

"I just couldn't sit and wait for you to call."

"Why?"

"I don't know. I just couldn't do it."

"What is it, some man thing?"

"I don't know. It was after that Saturday surgery I told you about. I really wanted you to be home when I got here and you weren't and I was pissed."

"So you figured you'd have dinner with your old girlfriend and get back at me?"

"Basically, but it wasn't thought out. I just called her up—"

"I didn't even know she was in New York. Did you know all the time that she was here?"

"No, I ran into her at Jeff and Laura's housewarming—"

"She was there? How'd she know them?"

"Turns out she and Laura knew each other from some camp."

"Oh. This is unbelievable, Jack."

I sat on the edge of the bed, absorbing it all.

"So, do you believe that little Miss Perfect would actually go through this alone? Be a single mother?"

"I don't know. It's completely out of character. I don't know what she's gonna do. I do know she's not going to force me to marry her. I want you, and I've made that clear to her."

"What are you talking about?"

"Well, when she called this afternoon to tell me that she'd told you, I told her then that I was still planning to marry you, if you'd still have me. I told her that I love you more than she'd ever know—"

"I can't even, I can't even think about that now. I need some time away from you. I need to leave for a while, a few days or weeks, until I figure out what I want to do."

"I don't think we should separate now—"

"I don't give a fuck what you think—"

"Alice?"

"I'm going to my place."

"Stay here, this is your home, too. I'll leave—"

"Fine."

"I'll go stay at Jeff's—"

"I don't care where you go, you've just got to get outta my sight."

DISAPPOINTMENT had become such a part of all my relationships, the absence of it had made this one seem unreal. My first relationship, with my brother, had been sweet and tight, and then he'd turned into something else when he'd tried to hurt me. Sidney had disappeared from my life after he'd chosen to be a woman. Abdul was a fraud, as was Miles. I was getting better, though, I realized. Even though Jack had done a horrible thing, it didn't feel like the same kind of betrayal. The kind where it became obvious that you were in love with a phantom. That the person you were involved with was completely different from what you thought. This wasn't that kind of letdown. The thing that I'd uncovered about Jack was that he was amazingly naive.

The morning after I found out that Jack had gotten Sherry pregnant, I felt numb. The idea that he had slept with her pissed me off, but it was going to take time to find an emotion to match how I felt about the pregnancy. I had felt, all along with Jack, that something was too perfect, that something was going to happen to fuck things up. It was like I'd been waiting for him to fuck up in a way that was familiar to me. Everything had been too neat and tidy: nice apartment, appropriate profession. Now something had happened, a mar, and I should've been depressed, in bed listening to some Vivaldi on WQXR with the covers over my head. Instead I stood in my bright white kitchen in my bright white terry-cloth robe, staring at the kitchen sink, the dirty sponge and the ratty rubber gloves hanging over the faucet, trying to decide between Jamaican blue mountain and Java City house blend. I should've thrown away those rubber gloves, but I always did have a problem disconnecting from things. I saved everything, remembered everything—pieces of conversations on the bus to day camp, slights from my freshman high school English teacher, Miles. I couldn't seem to completely sever that relationship. I thought I had. Jack accepted me, all of me, good, bad, insecure, uptight, lazy, moody me. Miles didn't. But I never ached for Jack the way I had for Miles, never bounced up and down in the backseat of a cab, so excited just to be with Jack, the way I had for Miles. "It's just lust, you can't live on lust," Cheryl would chant whenever I attempted to talk to her about Miles. I knew she was right, but sometimes I wanted to just give in to lust, believe that it was a symbol of something deeper between Miles and me. I felt warring factions inside—the rational and the romantic. Aunt Thelma had had three husbands, married all of them 'cause she was crazy, passionately, in love. "Wouldn't do it again," she'd said.

I needed to call Miles to apologize for yesterday. He'd want to know what happened with Jack. I poured blue mountain into my mug, stirred in the half-and-half, and checked the kitchen clock. At seven-thirty Miles would already have been at his desk for an hour and a half. I needed to get into the shower and get ready for work. I picked up the cordless that was sitting on the kitchen counter.

"Hey, babe, how ya doin' today?" Miles said. I pictured him with that mouthpiece wrapped on one side of his face, wearing a pair of silly, expensive suspenders.

"Hi, I'm fine. Listen, I'm sorry about yesterday."

"Oh, baby, you don't have to apologize for that. I should've known better."

"Thanks for being so understanding."

"So what happened when you got home?"

"We talked and I told him I needed to be alone for a while."

"You put the man outta his own place? Damn, Alice."

"No, he volunteered to leave."

"Baby, that's cold. So was he repented or what?"

"Yeah, I guess."

"So whatcha gone do?"

"I don't know."

"So, you wanna meet me for dinner later?"

When Miles smelled blood, he stalked the vein.

"Okay."

"Cool. I'll meet you at Barney's, downtown, at seven—"

"Why Barney's?"

•

"I just need to exchange something. It'll take two seconds, then we can go next door to Le Madri and have some dinner. Okay. Listen. I gotta hop."

"Miles, wait a minute. I'll just meet you at Le Madri."

"Okay. Later."

I pushed the Out button, took a swig of coffee, and wrote "7pm Le Madri" on the kitchen counter pad.

When it opened, Le Madri became an immediate hot restaurant. Its ambiance was that of most hip Manhattan eateries. It was big, noisy, and sparsely designed in a Greco-Roman fashion. The maître d', Paolo, wore his long brown hair slicked back into a ponytail and an Armani-esque suit, but his accent was more Bay Ridge than Bologna. As usual, Miles was late and had instructed Paolo to seat me and start on the Cristal, which was already chilling at the table. I followed Paolo to a corner table, my left suede pump pinching my pinkie toe. I was wearing work clothes, my blue wool crepe trouser suit over a hidden black lace camisole. I sat down, watched Paolo pour me a perfect flute of champagne, and pulled out some work manuscripts to read through while I waited for Miles. Before I'd finished one, Miles came bustling toward the table. He shook Paolo's hand as if they were old friends, sat down, breathless, and leaned over to kiss my cheek. "Hey, baby, I'm sorry I'm late. You been here long?"

"Nope, believe it or not I just got here about five minutes ago," I said, stuffing the manuscripts back into my black leather tote.

"Good. I wanted to be here when you got here, but I got tied up—"

"Yeah, I know the drill. Another deal that wouldn't close."

"You know the drill, baby. You look beautiful. I like what you're doing with your hair."

"Miles, my hair is the same."

"Oh yeah? It looks different."

"So why the champagne?"

"I know you like it, so, you know, it's just like old times. What should we drink to? How about you and me?"

I shifted from my right to my left buttock and looked around the restaurant. There was a woman to my left with a large blond do, checking us out. She quickly averted her stare when I looked at her.

"Let's drink to my new job."

"You have a new job? When did that happen?"

"Couple months ago. I'm a senior editor at *View*."

"Well then, go, girl, let's drink to your new job and your new man." Miles raised his glass.

"Miles, I—"

"I know, baby, you don't want to drink to me, that's all right. We have time."

I had downed my first glass and was mostly finished with my second when I looked up and saw what I thought must have been virtual reality.

Paolo was escorting Jack to our table. Jack was smiling. Miles was slouching in his chair, sipping champagne and looking, blankly, at Jack coming toward us.

"Hi, sweetie," Jack said.

"Jack? What are you doing here?"

Miles sat upright, put his glass down on the table, and ran his hand down his shirt to smooth his tie.

"Hi, you're Miles, right? I'm Jack." He extended his hand, then pulled a seat from the blond woman's table and sat down. "So, did you guys order yet?"

Miles and I were both too stunned to speak. We just sat looking at Jack as if we might be witnessing him have a breakdown. He was acting as though nothing were wrong, as if the three of us were just all old friends, instead of Miles being my former lover. I was afraid he might be losing it, so I decided not to say anything much. It seemed that Miles decided the same thing.

The waiter came over with a flute for Jack, poured, and took our order.

"So, Jack," Miles said, recovering from his minicoma, "you're a doctor, I hear."

"Um, yes, a surgeon. I'm over at Mt. Sinai. And you're in finance?"

"Investment banking. I buy companies, break 'em up, sell 'em or put 'em together. It's mergers and acquisitions, M and A."

"So do you have any work these days? Seems like M and A's went out with the boom-boom eighties—"

"Naw, they ain't over, it's just that we're doin' bitness the way it was before the go-go years."

I looked at them incredulously: go-go, boom-boom, two grown men discussing billions of dollars in baby talk.

I cut in. "So, Jack, how'd you know I was here?"

"You wrote it down . . . on the pad . . . near the phone."

"Oh yeah, right."

I tried to figure out a polite way to ask him what the hell he was doing here but couldn't. We ate our dinner in inconsequential chatter. Jack dominated the conversation, talking on and on about hematomas and other medical procedures that he'd done recently. He caressed my hand across the table, as if things between us were just fine. We left the restaurant without dessert. Outside, on Seventh Avenue, Jack turned to Miles and shook his hand. He pulled me toward him, grabbing my hand with one of his, hailing a cab with the other.

•

"Thanks for dinner," I yelled over my shoulder to Miles, who, as usual, had insisted on picking up the check.

"Driver, can you take the West Side Highway, please, to Eighty-fifth and Central Park West."

He settled back in the seat, looking like a cat after a run-in with some field mice.

"What are you doing, Jack, coming in there like that?"

"I'm showing you that I have no intention of letting you get away."

"And where are we going? Who lives at Eighty-fifth and CPW?"

"I have a surprise for you, or have I done enough of that for one night?"

"Yeah, that was a surprise, seeing you come hoppin' in there like that. Miles practically swallowed his tongue when I introduced you."

"He should've. He's not for you. I hope you're not seriously thinking about leaving me."

"I don't know what I'm going to do."

"I'll do anything you say, Alice. Whatever you want, I'll do."

"You said you saw Le Madri written on a pad. What were you doing in the apartment?"

"Getting some shirts. I was going to head to Jeff's, but then I figured I'd go to the restaurant."

"Oh, really?"

"I wanted to see you and tell you that I love you and we can work this out."

The cab pulled up to the northwest curb of Central Park West at Eighty-fifth Street. While Jack paid the driver, I got out and checked my hair in a brass plate that provided the building's address.

•

"I don't want to go to a party."

"We're not going to a party."

"Well, why are we here?"

"Give me your hand."

I let Jack pull me through the ornate lobby of the huge prewar building. The doorman, who was dressed in a gray uniform trimmed in black braid, greeted Jack by name.

"How does he know you? Who lives here?" I was getting annoyed.

We got into the walnut-paneled elevator and rode up to the fifteenth floor, where there were only two apartments. Jack took keys out of his pocket, inserted them into the lock, and flicked on the lights. "Ta-da."

The light came from a gold sconce. I looked around at a large, empty, newly painted room with perfect waxed parquet floors.

"So what's up? Whose place is this?"

Jack took both of my hands and held them in his. "It's yours. I bought it for us."

"NO, HE DIDN'T JUST come in the restaurant and claim yo ass."

"Yes. He did. It was like what's-his-name in *An Officer and a Gentleman,* when he comes in the factory and picks up Debra Winger and carries her off."

"Well, he didn't pick you up, let's not get carried away."

Cheryl and I both laughed.

"I haven't even told you the best part."

"There's more. I can't stop smilin' at picturing ol' Miles standing there gettin' outdone."

"There's more."

•

I told her about the apartment.

"Damn. Three bedrooms, Central Park West. We're talkin' half mil, easy."

"Probably more."

"What're you gonna do?"

"I don't know. I mean, this baby thing. He cheated on me."

"Yeah, I know, it's fucked. But—"

"I know what you're gonna say—"

"Now, how you figure that—"

" 'Cause you're so damn materialistic."

"Oh, and you're not?"

"We're not talking about me."

"But we are. So which bothers you more, that he slept with someone else, that he slept with Sherry, or that she's pregnant?"

"How about all of the above?"

"Pick one."

"I guess that she's pregnant. I could get over the cheating, I think. I could probably be convinced that he wouldn't do it again. He seems really sorry, but a baby—"

"What is it, that the kid is a reminder that he cheated or that you wanted to be the one to have his baby?"

"Yeah. I wanted us to have kids together—"

"So you can still have kids together—"

"But it won't be the same. It won't be his first, plus I don't want to be a stepmother."

"Maybe you won't see the kid. Who says you have to?"

"If we're married, the kid'll come to our house."

"Not if you don't wanna see him—"

"Well, I couldn't—"

"You're always talking about what you couldn't. Let's talk about what you can. You can say who comes and who doesn't come in your house."

"Well, I don't know. I mean, I'd be a stepmother, I'm not sure I wanna be one."

"But think about that apartment—"

"Yeah, it's nice, but I don't want to feel bought—"

"Oh, please, we all are. At least your price is higher than most—"

"You are so cynical. When did you get so jaded?"

"When I came home to an empty-ass apartment, I guess."

"He was an asshole, one with bad dental work."

"True, but I worked overtime to pay for his sorry ass to go to law school."

"A misjudgment—"

"An expensive one, but back to you—"

"I don't know, maybe if he'd done something more romantic than buying me an apartment—"

"You'd rather have flowers than real estate? You've really got problems."

"Not flowers, I mean, I don't know. Something more heartfelt."

"Like . . . ?"

"Like a ring. I never did get an engagement ring."

"Mmmm. A ring. Now we wouldn't be talking about any old stone in a piece of gold, would we? I hope you're talkin' Liz Taylor rock?"

"Nothing that gaudy. Something nice."

"Then you'd forgive him?"

"Cheryl, I don't know. I don't know what to do."

"What does your therapist say?"

"You know, 'What do you want to do?' "

"She's a big help."

•

"She actually is, but ultimately it's all up to me. You know they don't tell you what to do."

"I know, but isn't she supposed to help you get to where you want to be?"

"Yeah, and she's done that. I know I know what I want to do. The question really is, do I have the courage."

"You so deep."

We laughed again.

"Well, whatever you decide, you know I'm here."

"I know."

"I think Jack is guilty, but not of being a dog, just of being stupid enough to go to her house."

"You think?"

"Yeah, it doesn't make any sense otherwise. I mean, he'd had her. He probably could've had her anytime he wanted, before you or during you. So why suddenly does he have to fuck her?"

"So you really think he went over there to just have dinner?"

"Basically. Maybe a little flirting, but not to have sex."

"You know, I know that Jack isn't a dog—"

"So forgive the man and get on with it."

"You're so cut and dry."

"Yeah, and I should get my cut-and-dried ass off the phone. My phone bill, this time, you know."

"All right. Love you."

"Right back."

I hung up the phone and looked around the apartment. It was a Sunday afternoon and I was really missing Jack. He'd been staying at Jeff's for almost three weeks, and I hadn't seen him since the night he showed me the apartment. It was a gorgeous place.

• • •

The walls, the furniture, and the floor of *View*'s waiting area were all white trimmed in gold. My office was big enough for a large desk, a small computer desk, a couch, and two small white leather chairs. I had a glass door. As I walked toward my office I could see that it looked like a florist's, and my assistant, Stacy, was holding a vase, trying to find a clear surface to put it on. Stacy was just out of Bard, wore chocolate lipstick, and looked down a lot.

"Stacy, what is all of this?"

The smell was transcendental.

"Um, oh hi, Alice. You got all of these. There're eleven of them. I counted."

"What?"

There were flowers everywhere. Six black tubular vases on my desk and one in each chair, three on the floor.

"Here's the card."

She handed me a small envelope. It read: "If this doesn't work . . . I'm desperate without you. J"

Stacy seemed embarrassed and hurried to leave my office. "If you want me to do something with them—"

"No, that's okay. Thanks, Stacy."

I closed my door and wished that it weren't glass. I threw my bag on my couch and sat at my desk. I smiled even though I didn't want to. There were red ones and yellow and pretty coral ones, pale pinks, and ivory ones.

I rubbed my face and decided I needed to order breakfast, a bagel and some decaf. I read through the papers while waiting for my food to arrive. When the in-house phone rang, I grabbed my wallet to pay the delivery person. When I got to the lobby Jack was standing there.

"I miss you."

•

"Yeah, I gather that." I looked around for a delivery person.

"Alice, please let me come back home. I'm sick without you."

"Uh-huh."

"Don't you miss me?"

"Yeah, I miss you."

"So let me come home. Let's go on with our lives."

"Like nothing happened? Look, let's go to my office."

He followed me through a maze of cubicles. I shut my door behind him, and he moved a vase and sat down.

"Looks nice in here. Smells good, too—"

"Yeah. Thanks for the flowers."

"You're welcome."

"So, you wanna just pick up like nothing happened?"

"No, that's not what I'm saying. Something has happened, I fucked up, but it shouldn't be the end of us."

"Hmmm, and what about the baby? I don't know if I want to be a stepmother."

"I know we can work it out."

"And what about Sherry bothering us all the time?"

"After a while, I'm sure that won't happen. Please, Alice."

"Jack, you know, you really hurt me. I trusted you."

"I know, and I swear I'll never cheat on you again, ever. I'll never put myself in a compromising position. I promise, Alice."

A knock on the glass interrupted us.

"My God, what's going on in here? Did somebody die or give birth?"

"Holly, this is Jack, um, Jack Russworm. Jack Russworm, Holly Thomasson."

"Oh, hi, Jack. It's so nice to meet you. I've heard a lot about you." Holly extended one hand and held the other to her neck.

"Nice meeting you. You have a nice operation here, very impressive," he said.

"Thanks. So why all the flowers?"

There was no response.

"Alice, whatever it is, say yes. Nice meeting you, Jack. See ya later, Alice."

Holly left and closed the door. As soon as Holly was out of sight Jack and I turned and looked at each other and let out a hoot.

CLAIR SAT ON THE living room floor, wrapping our heavy green wineglasses in newspaper. Jack was downstairs with the movers, who had already loaded the big stuff, the leather sofa, the grandma chair, bookcases, the pine desk. It was a bright cool late spring day.

"So, dear, do you like your new place?" Clair began.

"I love it. It's gorgeous, and best of all, it's on the West Side. You haven't seen it yet?"

"No, Jack hasn't had time to take me by there. I'll see it today, when you all go over. If that's okay?"

•

"Oh, of course, I'll even give you lunch."

"So tell me about it."

"It's beautiful and huge, twice as big as this place, and bright. We have a southeastern view of the park, the sun will be great for my African violets. There are two huge marble bathrooms, the kitchen is an eat-in with a mahogany island and cabinets. There are two walk-in closets, one in the master bedroom, and a washer and dryer."

"It sounds just perfect. I was so surprised, you know, that Jack picked it out by himself."

"I couldn't believe it, either."

"Well, dear, I'm just so pleased things are still on track."

"So Jack told you about all that, huh?"

"Oh yes, dear, he told me. Poor thing, he was just devastated. Who would have ever thought that Sherry, from such a good family, would pull something like that? It's just so—" Clair stopped herself.

"Ghetto?" I heard myself say.

"Uh, well, yes. I mean—"

"I know, girls from Connecticut, whose fathers are doctors, don't behave that way—"

In therapy, I had been learning to say what I thought. Clair was clearly taken aback, but as a woman in her sixties she was on a similar mission and appreciated my honesty.

"Yes, it's such a shock, and I understand that she's planning to keep the child. Is that really true?"

I sighed and nodded.

"Well, she can't possibly know what a mistake she's making, it's hard enough raising a child with two parents present."

"Yeah, well. Jack and I met with a friend of ours who's a financial consultant, and he's drawing up a package for the baby."

"And what about a will?"

"We have to see a lawyer about that."

It wasn't the vision I had dreamed of when I thought about getting married. I had pictured myself shopping for a dress, registering for gifts, deciding on the flowers, not worrying about my husband-to-be's newborn and about becoming a stepmother, or a "stepmonster," as the kid will undoubtedly think of me. Aunt Thelma always told me life is never presented in a nice, neat package, and if it is, be wary.

Jack walked into the apartment with sweat glistening on his forehead and his gray sweatshirt smudged with something that looked like grease. His old khakis were so worn around the waist that his beeper was literally hanging on by a thread. A big toe was beginning to peek through his Tretorns. He looked adorable.

"Hey, Mother. How ya doin' there? You okay on the floor like that?"

"I'm fine, dear. How's the packing, are we just about ready to go?" Clair said from her pillowed perch.

We both looked to Jack for an answer, and I surveyed the apartment for myself to estimate how much longer before I could say good-bye to this place that had never felt like home.

"They've got all the major stuff on the truck, so they should be ready to take off in a few minutes. I'm going to get the car and I'll meet you two in front, okay, Alice?"

Our new oversized cream-colored linen sofa and love seat and floral damask armchair had been delivered and were still wrapped in plastic, sitting in the middle of our new home. Clair, Jack, and I carried small boxes of plants, toilet paper, phones, and towels.

"Oh my. This place is spectacular. It's simply beautiful," Clair said, putting her box down on a windowsill. "Oh, let me just look around."

•

She went from room to room, oohing and ahhing all the way. Jack and I stood in the living room and looked at each other.

"Come here, you."

I went to him and we held on to each other.

"Do you know how much I love you?" Jack said.

I wanted to cry. "Me too."

"It's gonna be great for us, Alice."

We kissed each other the way we used to. I silently wished I felt convinced.

Clair found us embraced. "You know you two— Oh, sorry."

We disconnected and turned toward her.

"You know, you could have the wedding right here. It would be perfect."

"Mmmm, yeah, we could do that. Whaddya think, Jack?"

"Whatever you want, sweetie."

"So have you two set a date?"

"Well, we've talked about Memorial Day weekend," I said.

"Memorial Day! Jack, the Russworms won't like that. Besides, it's a month from now!" Clair exclaimed.

"Yeah, well, they'll just have to put off going to the Vineyard for one weekend. I want her as my wife as soon as possible."

"Well, Alice, I guess we have our work cut out," Clair said.

I went downstairs, walked to Broadway to get sandwiches and potato salad, beer and seltzer. I believed that Jack wouldn't cheat on me again, or at least I tried to make myself believe it. I did know one thing. We had to just play it all the way out. We had as good a chance of surviving as anybody else. There's always going to be some problem, I told myself.

Jack and his mom both had beers with lunch and became chattier by the bottle.

•

"So, Jack, dear, have you talked to the Steptoes at all since this happened?"

"Actually, no, I haven't. I wasn't sure how to handle that, frankly, Mother."

"Well, what is Sherry saying? What did she say when you told her that you were still going to marry Alice?"

I had never asked him that question.

"You know, Sherry can be pretty abusive. During this whole thing, she's been pretty nasty and said some crazy stuff. One time she threatened to sue me and make a big scandal, then she threatened to get some guys to beat me up. She's not used to not getting her way."

"I can't believe she threatened you. So when was the last time you heard from her?" Clair pressed on.

"A few weeks ago. She's calmed down since the time she asked me to do Lamaze with her."

Clair's eyes bugged out, and I almost choked.

"Lamaze? She wants you to do birthing class with her? What did you say?" I finally asked.

"Alice, what do you think? I said no, of course, I feel horrible about it, you know, the idea of her doing it all alone."

"She'll find somebody to do it with her. She won't be alone. I can't believe she'd ask you to do that. She's not going to give up," I said.

Suddenly a vision came into my mind: Sherry in beautiful lingerie, looking like Glenn Close in *Fatal Attraction.*

"She doesn't seem to be letting up," Clair said.

"Jack, we're gonna have to think of something to keep her in check," I said.

"You mean, like hire a hit man." Jack laughed.

•

"I'm serious, I think we have to—"

"Alice, dear, perhaps she'll just stop on her own. If you do something, that'll just provoke her. Chances are if you ignore her, she'll tire and leave you be," Clair said. "You two must show a united front. She has to see your relationship as solid as a brick wall and that nothing she can do will cause a crack. That's my advice to you as marrieds for all outsiders. Once she realizes that, she'll have to go away. I mean, after all, the girl isn't insane."

Jack and I looked at each other. The brick wall had conjured a nice image, one that I'd never even considered; it was outside my expectations.

•

MY MOTHER WORE an elegant apple-green silk suit. Every few years, she bought, instead of made, a new outfit. It was usually something simple: a wool jersey dress, a pants suit. A contrast to her home creations. For this occasion, Aunt Thelma introduced her to Bergdorf's. "She said she had to have something special for your day. I ain't never seen your mama so nervous," Aunt Thelma confided to me after their shopping trip.

The air on holidays always seemed different. Maybe it was just the stillness from the collective relaxation.

•

Jack's relatives, who usually opened their summer homes on the Vineyard during Memorial Day, had moaned and groaned when we announced that we were getting married at the end of May. They considered our choice blasphemous and told us as much.

Cheryl had come up a week early to help me get things arranged. The four of us, Jack and I, Cheryl and Jeff, who'd met only once before, went out for an informal rehearsal dinner at Vince and Eddie's the night before the wedding. I was secretly hoping that Cheryl and Jeff would like each other, and they did, but like buddies. They'd each pronounced separately that they were not the other's type.

Jack and I spent the morning apart. He and Jeff went for a run in Central Park and uptown to get haircuts. Cheryl and I lounged in our bathrobes, drank coffee, and talked. She'd said, uncharacteristically, that she thought it was poetic, us getting married in our new space. Neither of us had slept much the night before. I felt both euphoric and scared, happy for the relationship and our beautiful new home and scared of making a mistake. Sherry would always be a part of our lives through the baby. We had a trust set up for the baby as well as money put away for monthly expenses. That would put a small dent in our monthly income.

Cheryl hired her friend Barry, whom she knew from Atlanta, to decorate the living room for the wedding. He lived in New York now and was a window designer at Barney's.

"Alice, this is a fierce apartment," Barry said after looking around. He had borrowed several golden and copper urns from work to hold the pale French tulips. He put up ivory raw silk drapes, which were covered with golden stars, and gathered the drapes with large gold tassel tiebacks to give the apartment "a funky movie set look." I loved it more than the place I had reserved and lost $500 on.

•

We hired a caterer who specialized in southern and West Indian food. There was fish chowder and corn bread with jalapeño peppers, callaloo, macaroni and cheese, shrimp Creole, collard greens, oyster stuffing, and a turkey. We had a chocolate liqueur buttercream wedding cake with a brown-faced bride and groom on top. A bar was set up in our long foyer, and the buffet table was in the kitchen. We had a tubful of Perrier-Jouët on ice.

While Barry and Cheryl helped the caterer set things up, Jack came back to get me to go for a walk.

"Mmmm, that boy is fine," I heard Barry mutter to Cheryl. I went in the bedroom and pulled on a pair of leggings and a shirt.

Outside, Jack reached for my hand as we headed across the street, toward the park. "I want to show you something."

"Our last walk as single people," I said aloud, to myself.

"How 'bout that." Jack turned around and hugged me.

It was cool for late May, and I wished I had worn a sweater. I wanted to go back inside, have tea and soak in the tub, and try to convince myself that this was just another day, but Jack steered me to a bench, where we both sat down.

"Aren't you cold?" I said, eyeing him. He was dressed in a thin tank, running shorts, and a hooded sweatshirt, unzipped.

"No. I'm okay. I have something—"

He reached into his sweatshirt pocket and pulled out a small blue velvet ring box. We had never gotten around to shopping for an engagement ring. We never could come to any agreement as to how to go about it. Jack didn't want me to go along, and I didn't know what I wanted. My heart started beating fast. Suppose I didn't like what he had picked out? What would I say? What I felt always showed on my face.

"Alice," Jack said, trying to look appropriately serious but looking goofy instead, "will you wear this ring and be my wife?"

•

We smiled at each other, eyes filled with tears. He handed me the box, and I opened it.

"It's your mother's ring."

"Yes, and before that, it was my grandmother's. My mother wanted you to have it."

I took it out of the case and held it, tilting it so that it picked up the light. "Here, you put it on me."

"I love you very much. Thank you for becoming my wife."

"It's beautiful, Jack. I love it and I love you."

"So, you'll marry me, then?"

When we got back to the apartment Barry and Cheryl and the caterers were all set up. Aunt Thelma, my mother and father, and Clair had arrived and were in the living room, talking. I was glad Cheryl was there. Clair and my parents hadn't met before, and I was sure that they'd all be tense. Cheryl would put everybody at ease. Jeffrey was taking a shower.

"Well, where the hell have you two been? Alice, you're not even dressed," Aunt Thelma started.

"Give me a kiss," I said to her.

We pecked on the mouth and she kept on talking. "This place is sayin' somethin'."

I kissed my mom and dad.

"So I see you've all met."

They all nodded and smiled self-consciously.

"Look, I brought you this for somethin' old. It was your grandma's," Aunt Thelma said, pulling an intricate pink lace slip from a Macy's shopping bag.

"Oh, it's so pretty," I said, holding it up. "Look—" I stuck out my hand, remembering the ring. "Look at what Jack gave me."

"Nice," Aunt Thelma said, holding my hand toward the sunlight. "Now, let's get you dressed."

•

"Clair, thank you." Clair and I walked toward each other and hugged.

"You're more than welcome," Clair said, hugging me hard.

"Alice, you've got like an hour before folks start gettin' here," Cheryl said.

I had found the perfect ivory damask suit, with a low-cut big collar, fitted waist jacket, and a little straight skirt. Aunt Thelma, in her ever-present sunglasses, thought a pearl-and-crystal choker was the only jewelry I needed. A makeup artist that we used for shoots at the magazine did my makeup and put my hair up, after I had a quick shower.

Cheryl wore a burnt orange sheath of heavy silk with matching sexy, high-heeled Manolo Blahnik pumps that she'd found on sale, but still cost plane fare from Atlanta. She walked out ahead of me to the strains of Bach for the violin coming from our CD player. Both of us carried delicate bouquets of white and pink roses and freesia. Jack and Jeffrey wore dark blue suits with freesia boutonnieres. Jack shifted his weight and looked distinguished. The fashion photographer's motor drive was all I heard.

The straightforward civil ceremony was quick. "With this ring . . ." I slipped a narrow gold band onto Jack's finger. He surprised me and put a band of circular diamonds over my new antique ruby.

We were pronounced husband and wife, and Aunt Thelma popped a bottle of champagne.

ABOUT THE AUTHOR

Benilde Little was born and raised in Newark, New Jersey, graduated from Howard University, and did graduate work at Northwestern University. She has worked for the Newark *Star-Ledger, People,* and *Essence.* She lives in suburban New York City with her husband and their daughter.